PENGUIN BOOKS
AN ORDINARY TALE ABOUT WOMEN AND OTHER STORIES

Fatimah Busu is an award-winning Malaysian novelist, short-story writer, and academic. Born in 1943 in Kampung Pasir Pekan, Kelantan, she is considered one of the most formidable Malay women writers of her generation. Her award-winning short stories include *Mawar Yang Belum Gugur* (1971), *Nasinya Tumpah* (1972), and *Anak-anak dari Kampung Pasir Pekan* (1975). Her first novel, *Ombak Bukan Biru*, was published to acclaim in 1977, and was followed by other notable novels, including *Kepulangan* (1980) and *Salam Maria* (2004).

Fatimah is also known for her essays on comparative literature and literary criticism. Fatimah is the recipient of several literary awards including the Kelantan State Laureate in 2015. She rejected the prestigious SEA Write Award as a protest against the violence against Muslim communities in South Thailand. Fatimah is considered a somewhat controversial figure by mainstream literary circles, for her strong views and acute portrayals of the inner contradictions of Malay society.

Pauline Fan is a writer, literary translator, and cultural researcher. She is creative director of cultural organization PUSAKA and currently serves as adjunct professor at the Faculty of Modern Languages and Communication at Universiti Putra Malaysia. Pauline was director of the

George Town Literary Festival (2019 to 2023) and is a founding-curator of KALAM—Confluence of Writers & Ideas, a literary gathering in Kuala Lumpur.

Pauline's translation of poems by Sarawak poet Kulleh Grasi, *Tell Me, Kenyalang* (Circumference Books, 2019), was shortlisted in the United States for the National Translation Award in Poetry and longlisted for the Best Translated Book Awards in 2020.

Pauline's literary translations from German to Malay include works by Immanuel Kant, Rainer Maria Rilke, and Paul Celan. She holds a Masters in German Literature from the University of Oxford.

ADVANCE PRAISE FOR *AN ORDINARY TALE ABOUT WOMEN AND OTHER STORIES*

'Reading Fatimah Busu's stories feels like unwrapping a surprise gift of rare beauty. As you journey through her words, you can almost touch the leaves, hear the roar of hurricanes, and see the remarkable Malay women draped in sarongs. Here, nature is not merely a backdrop; it speaks as a narrator in its own right. This is one of the most enchanting aspects of Fatimah's storytelling: her structure defies traditional narrative, granting voices to trees, animals, children, and the marginalized. These stories are profound and stirring, and in Pauline Fan's brilliant translation, they find their perfect place.'

—Jokha Alharthi, Omani author and winner of the 2019 International Booker Prize

'Fatimah Busu's works illuminate overlooked realities in a world predominantly shaped and defined by male storytellers. These 'ordinary tales' delve into the lives of ordinary women—mothers, daughters, sisters, lovers, wives—whose voices have been buried alive, deep beneath the surface of Asian homes. These are stories of half the world's population, unharmed yet unheard, unseen, and unspoken. They capture emotions and experiences that have yet to be named, existing outside the framework of male-dominated narratives. Mellow, nuanced, full of flavour—and brought to life through a truly excellent translation—Fatimah Busu's stories offer a profound and deeply moving reading experience.'

—Veeraporn Nitiprapha, Thai author,
winner of S.E.A Write Award 2015 and 2018

'Fatimah Busu, a renowned novelist from Kelantan, draws deeply from her home state, known for its cultural uniqueness and identity. It is in this cultural background that her stories are rooted and have bloomed. Her use of the Malay language is masterful and sensitive, not least, because of the Kelantanese elements and the musicality of its expression.

Writing since the 1960s, Fatimah has produced an impressive body of short stories, novels, and criticism. To date she is the most prolific and the most open to new ideas and literary experimentation. She digs deep into the realities of contemporary Malaysian women, offering her perspective to this special area of Malaysian life.

The publication of *An Ordinary Tale About Women and Other Stories* by Penguin Random House SEA, evocatively translated by Pauline Fan, opens a window to the world, making Fatimah Busu's distinct voice accessible to an international readership. This outstanding collection affirms the transformative power of translation, ensuring that the wisdom and artistry of Malay storytelling resonate far beyond our shores.'

—Prof. Muhammad Haji Salleh,
National Literary Laureate of Malaysia

An Ordinary Tale About Women and Other Stories

Fatimah Busu

Translated from Malay by

Pauline Fan

PENGUIN BOOKS

An imprint of Penguin Random House

PENGUIN BOOKS

Penguin Books is an imprint of the Penguin Random House group of
companies whose addresses can be found at
global.penguinrandomhouse.com

Published by Penguin Random House SEA Pte Ltd
40 Penjuru Lane, #03-12, Block 2
Singapore 609216

First published in Penguin Books by Penguin Random House SEA 2024

Translation Copyright © Pauline Fan 2024

Cover art credit *Woman Bathing In A Stream, After Rembrandt - Perempuan
Mandi di Sungai, Selepas Rembrandt*, from National Visual Art Collections,
National Art Gallery Malaysia, by Ismail Zain. 1968. Oil on board,
90.1 x 120.6 cm. BSLN1975.014.

All rights reserved

10 9 8 7 6 5 4 3 2 1

This is a work of fiction. Names, characters, places and incidents
are either the product of the author's imagination or are used fictitiously,
and any resemblance to any actual person, living or dead, events or
locales is entirely coincidental.

Please note that no part of this book may be used or reproduced in any manner
for the purpose of training artificial intelligence technologies or systems.

ISBN 9789815204667

Typeset in Garamond by MAP Systems, Bengaluru, India

This book is sold subject to the condition that it shall not, by way of trade
or otherwise, be lent, resold, hired out, or otherwise circulated without the
publisher's prior consent in any form of binding or cover other than that in
which it is published and without a similar condition including this condition
being imposed on the subsequent purchaser.

Contents

Introduction: Finding Fatimah Busu	ix
At the Edge of a River	1
An Ordinary Tale about Women	13
A Letter to Mother in Kampong Pasir Pekan	29
The Scrawny Cat	37
Spilled Rice	43
The Dowry of Desire	61
Watching the Full Moon	85
Watching the Rain	93
Narration of the Ninth Tale	101
The Lovers of Muharram	119

Introduction

Finding Fatimah Busu

I knew the name of Fatimah Busu long before I read any of her work. Her name would surface repeatedly in various writings on Malay literature, often spoken with reverence and admiration. It was clear that she was regarded as one of the great Malay writers of her generation, particularly as a master of the short story form. Yet, despite this recognition as a 'writer's writer', gathering Fatimah Busu's short stories for this collection was no small feat. Many of her works have been out-of-print for decades and are highly sought after in second-hand book circles in Malaysia. The scarcity of her collections made the task feel somewhat like a treasure hunt, each newly discovered story carrying a sense of rare victory.

In 2020, while curating the George Town Literary Festival—which took the form of podcasts in that year of pandemic and lockdown—I was determined to find Fatimah Busu and feature a special interview with her. With the kind assistance of National Laureate Professor Muhammad Haji

Salleh, I managed to track down the elusive writer. I called Fatimah on her landline and arranged to meet her at her home in Penang to personally invite her for the interview. She greeted me in a simple jubah and white headscarf, exuding a teacherly warmth that soon revealed sparks of mischievous humour. I was delighted when she agreed to participate in the podcast, which would be conducted in Malay and moderated by the Penang-based writer Regina Ibrahim.[1] At the end of our conversation, Fatimah gifted me her novel *Salam Maria* and graciously loaned me an out-of-print copy of one of her short story collections.

That very night, as I skimmed through Fatimah's book of short stories, one title immediately caught my eye: 'Kekasih Muharram'. The opening passages struck me deeply—I had never encountered anything quite like it in Malay fiction. I knew instantly that I wanted to translate Fatimah's work. I took photos of the pages of all the short stories that resonated with me. When I returned the book to Fatimah a few days later, I asked for her permission to translate her work into English, beginning with 'The Lovers of Muharram' ('Kekasih Muharram', 1977).[2]

---

[1] The podcast, 'Fatimah Busu: Memecah Tempurung Belenggu', can be listened to here: https://podcasters.spotify.com/pod/show/georgetownliteraryfest/episodes/Fatimah-Busu-Memecah-Tempurung-Belenggu-emsnhb

[2] An abbreviated version of 'The Lovers of Muharram', my translation of 'Kekasih Muharram', was published in Words Without Borders: *The Slow Burn of Inner Chaos: Writing from Malaysia*, co-edited by Adriana Nordin Manan and Pauline Fan, 2021.

Introduction

As I embarked on the process of selecting stories for this collection, I relied heavily on two main sources: Fatimah herself, who obligingly made photocopies of some stories, and the scattered network of second-hand booksellers across the country who became my allies in this search. One friend, Omar Bachok, a bookseller based in Johor, was particularly invaluable. I tasked him with the mission of hunting down Fatimah's work, and his perseverance paid off. He managed to unearth several rare anthologies published by Dewan Bahasa dan Pustaka in the early 1970s, in which some of Fatimah's prize-winning stories had been first published.

Through this meticulous and, at times, arduous process, I was able to piece together a selection of stories that reflects the breadth of Fatimah Busu's oeuvre. Each story in this collection is a testament to her mastery over her craft and her unyielding dedication to the art of storytelling. Translated into English for the first time, the short stories gathered here span Fatimah Busu's early work in 1960, her period of prolific writing in the 1970s, the peak of her creative powers in the 1980s, and her mature style in the 1990s. This collection features a few of her iconic early short stories, which won prizes in national literary competitions, and several lesser-known stories, which underscore her distinctive style and subject matter. The process of gathering them was like piecing together a mosaic, each fragment contributing to a fuller picture of Fatimah Busu's evocative fiction.

Subversion from the sidelines

Fatimah Busu's short stories are poignant narratives that capture often unheard and unseen realities within Malay society. Her work is frequently narrated from the perspective of children and adolescents, poor rural folk, and single mothers, offering vivid portrayals of lives vulnerable to the elements and subject to the whims of local authorities. One of the defining features of Fatimah Busu's work is her portrayal of 'everyday forms of resistance', as conceptualized by James C. Scott in *Weapons of the Weak: Everyday Forms of Peasant Resistance* (1985), his seminal study of farmers in Sedaka, Kedah. Fatimah's characters often engage in subtle, yet powerful, acts of defiance against the oppressive structures they face. These acts may not always be overt or revolutionary but are significant in their quiet assertion of agency and dignity.

Set predominantly in her hometown of Kampong Pasir Pekan, in the state of Kelantan in north-eastern Peninsular Malaysia, Fatimah Busu's early stories are saturated with local dialect and the minute details of everyday life. This regional specificity anchors her stories in a cultural and geographical context, imbuing them with authenticity while drawing readers into the textured reality of her characters. Her evocative depictions were influenced by her personal experience of growing up in poverty, raised primarily by her mother, with a father who was engaged in various forms of casual work and was seldom home. Narrated from a child's perspective,

Introduction

'At the Edge of a River' ('Di Tebing Sebuah Sungai', 1976) captures the realities of rural life in Kelantan through the communal effort of building a house. Exploring the capricious power wielded by local authorities, it offers a glimpse into the politics of land ownership as well as community spirit and resilience.

The characterization of Kelantanese village life is palpable in 'Spilled Rice' ('Nasinya Tumpah', 1972), one of Fatimah Busu's most iconic stories about rural children who accidentally consume poisonous mushrooms. The story's unflinching depiction of rural hardship, childhood innocence, and tragedy earned it a Hadiah Sastera prize from Dewan Bahasa dan Pustaka and led to its adaptation into a telemovie in 1986. Another story included here told from the perspective of children is 'The Scrawny Cat' ('Kucing Kurus', 1960)—a chilling portrayal of cruelty and regret. One of Fatimah Busu's earliest works, written when she was just sixteen years old, won her a consolation prize of RM60 in a children's story competition. Despite its disturbing theme, it was published in an anthology alongside works by established authors under the auspices of the Ministry of Education of Malaya.

Fatimah Busu's female characters possess strong subjectivity and agency, challenging the traditional boundaries of what women would be expected to write about in Malay literature. Her work disrupts the parameters of modern Malay literature that, at times, dismiss the writings of women as being prone to nostalgia, romance, and fantasy, incapable of addressing serious topics.

xiv   Introduction

Fatimah Busu courted controversy with her bold exploration of taboo subjects, such as sex and pregnancy out of wedlock, which diverged sharply from the dominant portrayals of women by her male contemporaries. Male Malay writers of her generation often depicted 'fallen women' or 'victimized women' through stereotypical tropes such as prostitutes, adulteresses, or good suffering wives. By contrast, Fatimah Busu's female characters are embedded in the local community and economy, engaged in work, and grappling with daily life. Offering a counter-narrative to the male-dominated literary landscape, she delves into the inner and outer struggles of her female characters with a complexity and nuance that renders them deeply human. In 'The Lovers of Muharram', Fatimah Busu portrays female desire and the devastating consequences of reckless love. This story stands out for its candid exploration of passion and its tragic aftermath, as well as the use of unconventional narrative form.

At the core of Fatimah Busu's stories is a strong undercurrent of social and political commentary. She deftly critiques structures of power and entrenched injustices, particularly focusing on the plight of women within Malay society. Her stories are deeply feminist, though not in the sense of Western, liberal feminism. Instead, she offers a critical perspective on the patriarchal systems and unjust legal frameworks that harshly penalize women for social ills. Through her narratives, she exposes the hypocrisy of ideological leaders who perpetuate such injustices while cloaking their actions in moralistic rhetoric. 'An Ordinary Tale about Women' ('Cerita Biasa

Introduction

Tentang Perempuan', 1996) exposes harsh realities faced by women: neglectful husbands, mistreated wives, rural girls who migrate to factory jobs in Penang only to fall prey to predatory men. This fearless story also addresses the severe punishments meted out to women for baby dumping and infanticide, offering a critical lens on gender dynamics and discrimination.

Fatimah Busu's formidable depiction of women is rooted in her Kelantanese origin. The centrality of women in traditional Kelantanese society is evident from their pervasive presence in Kelantan's mythology as well as in the local economy. The mythological landscape of Kelantan-Pattani is populated by female figures such as Che Siti Wan Kembang, a queen, and Puteri Sa'adong, a princess, who were powerful rulers of their kingdoms. In the mundane realm, the traditional role of women in Kelantan is one of household authority and economic power. While religious practice in Kelantan has been traditionally conservative, it also co-existed with traditional social values and local worldviews, in which women would play a dominant and highly visible role in community life. Even today, women wield more presence and power than men in the local markets of Kelantan and often manage the family expenses.

Another notable feature of Fatimah Busu's short fiction are her masterful reworkings and retellings of Malay *hikayats*, traditional epics, such as episodes from the *Sejarah Melayu (Malay Annals)*, *Hikayat Hang Tuah (The Epic of Hang Tuah)*, and *Hikayat Raja-raja Pasai (The Chronicles of Pasai)*. 'The Dowry of Desire' ('Mahar Asmara', 1984), audaciously reimagines the beloved legend of Puteri Gunung Ledang, exploring dark desire and the follies of power through the traditional tale. Puteri Gunung Ledang herself is portrayed not as a paragon of beauty and virtue, but a coquettish brat who relishes bringing the vainglorious Sultan Mahmud to madness and self-destruction. By contrast, 'Narration of the Ninth Tale' ('Alkisah Cetera yang Kesembilan', 1980), a retelling from the *Malay Annals*, delves into themes of loyalty, regret, and the passage of time. It contemplates the final days of Raja Malik ul-Mansur, who chooses to die beside the tomb of his loyal minister, Sidi Ali Hisyamuddin.

Fatimah Busu's literary oeuvre encompasses a convergence of styles and forms, blending realism, naturalism, magic realism, absurdism, and satire. Her narratives are imbued with dreams, flashbacks, stream of consciousness, and apocalyptic visions, often interwoven with local folklore and mythology. This syncretism of form and influence enables her to craft stories that are both deeply rooted in Malay culture and universally resonant. 'A Letter to Mother in Kampong Pasir Pekan' ('Surat untuk Emak di Kampung Pasir Pekan', 1980) is an embodiment of such syncretism. Written in epistolary form, this is a wild eschatological tale about a pestilence of *dajjal* ('deceivers') in the form of imp-like creatures running riot in the village. It blends supernatural and satirical elements to critique societal and moral decay.

Touches of magic realism and speculative fiction are prominent features in Fatimah Busu's storytelling. Alongside modernist influences, these tendencies are deeply rooted in old Malay epics and mythology, as well as the narrative traditions of Islamic mysticism. In her mature stories, the non-human world comes alive—birds, worms, and trees speak; a mother and son put on their wings and take flight—blurring the boundaries between reality and fantasy. This suspension of linear time and place creates a dreamlike quality that allows for profound explorations of both personal and societal issues, inviting readers into a realm where the mystical and the mundane coexist seamlessly.

In 'Watching the Rain' ('Melihat Hujan', 1994) a mother and child embark on a visionary and spiritual journey through the clouds, amidst a storm. The story blends mystical elements with deep philosophical musings—the protagonists reflect on the human condition and war, encountering single mother figures like Hajar, wife of the Prophet Ibrahim, and the Virgin Mary. 'Watching the Full Moon' ('Melihat Bulan Purnama', 1994) pairs stylistically and thematically with 'Watching the Rain'. As a mother and son watch the full moon rise over Teluk Bayan, they experience apocalyptic visions of humanity's moral decline. The story is a meditation on the loss of ethical values and dehumanization of society.

Restoring the light

Fatimah Busu's short stories are a powerful testament to the resilience and resourcefulness of the marginalized and the overlooked. She intricately weaves folklore, mysticism, and social critique, which provides a unique and fascinating lens through which to view the complexities of Malay society. Through her characters and their stories, she casts a light on those often unseen, illuminating their struggles, defiance, and enduring spirit. Her work is a crucial contribution to contemporary Malay literature, offering both a mirror to the society she depicts and a window into the universal human experience.

Despite her significant contributions to Malay literature, Fatimah Busu has been sidelined by the literary bureaucracy in the past few decades. Her feisty outspokenness, fearlessness in addressing social taboos, and unconventional narrative approach evidently made some quarters uneasy with her and her work. Her seminal novel, *Salam Maria*—a radical portrayal of a woman scorned by religious hypocrites who flees to the edge of the forest and establishes a spiritual sanctuary for outcast women— was rejected by Dewan Bahasa dan Pustaka, the national literary body of Malaysia. Some critics even accused the novel of being insulting to Islam, further contributing to her fall from favour. *Salam Maria* was eventually published independently in 2004; however, the novel was never as widely distributed as it deserved to be. That same year, Fatimah Busu rejected the highly coveted SEA Write Award in protest against the Tak Bai massacre in Thailand, in which eighty-five Thai Muslims lost their lives.[3]

---

[3] Haberkorn, Tyrell. 'In Bangkok: Remembering the Tak Bai Massacre.' *openDemocracy*, 3 November 2009, www.opendemocracy.net/en/in-bangkok-remembering-tak-bai-massacre/.

Introduction xix

This collection aims to redress the oversight of the literary bureaucracy by bringing Fatimah Busu's remarkable work to a wider audience. By restoring her rightful place in Malay literature, this collection not only honours Fatimah Busu's brilliance but also emphasizes the importance of radical voices in the literary landscape. It underscores the need to embrace subversive, unconventional writers who dare to challenge societal norms and push the boundaries of storytelling. Through Fatimah Busu's work, we are reminded of the transformative power of literature to shed light on the experiences of the disempowered and disenfranchised.

My translation attempts to capture the nuances of Fatimah Busu's prose, preserving the texture of her narrative voice and the vibrant cultural context of her settings. I hope to offer English-language readers an appreciation of the vivid imagery, emotional complexity, and cultural specificity that characterize her storytelling. The richness of her language, the idiosyncrasy of her style, the depth of her characters, and the sharpness of her social critique are vital elements that I have strived to bring to this translation.

This collection not only celebrates the literary achievements of a formidable Malaysian writer but also deepens the global understanding of Malay literature and the heterogenous voices within it. These stories offer readers an opportunity to experience the depth and diversity of the Malay experience through the literary imagination of one of its most compelling and original voices. By introducing Fatimah Busu's work to a new readership, we rekindle a light that has long been dimmed by neglect, in the hope that her legacy will burn brightly for generations to come.

—Pauline Fan
Kuala Lumpur, 14 August 2024

At the Edge of a River

The pulai trees are flowering in Kampong Pasir Pekan. Their acrid, heady scent elongates and merges with the moist night breeze, drifting over the entire lonely village.

Si Otik feels a silent fear creep into his heart with the pungent odour carried by the wind on this dark night among the murmuring leaves and branches.

Granny always associated the season of pulai flowers with tales of mischievous forest nymphs and of wayfarers who rove with long, gleaming *klewang* swords on moonless nights, tapping on the doors of village houses and casting terrifying curses.

'The house has no walls . . .' says Si Otik, 'no fence to dry clothes outside, no kitchen ledge . . . I'm frightened, Ma.'

Si Otik buries his face in his mother's bosom and curls up his small body against her belly. Siti clings to her mother's hips from behind, pressing her tummy against her mother's back.

'Tomorrow all the walls of the house will be up. It's just tonight there are no walls. Go to sleep . . .'

2   An Ordinary Tale About Women and Other Stories

Ma pulls the blanket over Otik's back. She knows he is spooked by the scent of pulai flowers.

'Tomorrow we'll call some people to help build the wall, ya—'

'What if something comes and creeps into the house tonight?'

'Cek is sleeping outside, no? Cek can strike at anything with his klewang . . . go to sleep. Don't be afraid, Otik. Kak Umi's here, Kak Siti's here . . . go to sleep now.'

And so, Si Otik falls asleep. And a dream emerges in his slumber.

* * *

As the reddish-gold rays of the rising sun flare over the riverbank on the other side, a swarm of people approach the house. Men. Women. Boys and girls. More and more of them come up through the dirt paths, single file in an endless stream. Their clothes are brightly coloured—the women cover their heads with seamless batik cloth in purple, yellow, green, blue, and red. The men wear their semutar headdress in red, yellow, green, white, and blue. Countless people arrive at the house. They build the walls, the rooms, the doors.

They toil away, their cheerful voices stirring a small commotion. As the sun climbs higher, even more people arrive. The place is strewn with piles of mixed cement, large stacks of beams, and joist wood, planed floor planks and wall boards.

At the Edge of a River

Soon, the house is finished. With many small rooms and compartments. Windows, doorways, staircases. Atop the high roof sits a cupola, like the dome of a mosque, adorned with the symbol of a moon and a star that glisten like red copper in the sunlight.

Then, everyone enters the house. Cek, Ma, Kak Umi, Kak Siti, Abang Mail, and Pakcik Yusof, the children, granny, deceased grandpa, departed Kak Bidah—everyone enters. And all the strangers who came streaming to help build the house, they all enter too. The house is brimming with people in every nook and cranny.

Gedegu! Si Otik hears a deafening, terrible sound. The house suddenly shatters, breaking apart into small pieces that go flying through the air. Walls, cement, roof, door-frames are hurled in every direction. Pillows and *kapok* fluff scatter all over the earth and grass. All the people who were inside the house run helter-skelter and turn into white ants, one can't differentiate men, women, and children. All ants. White floods through the dirt paths, scurrying aimlessly.

Little Otik calls out incessantly for Ma and Cek as he runs around naked, crying. But Ma and Cek have become white ants and who knows which dirt path they are on now. Who knows where Kak Kiah is too.

'Oh, all the people in the world have become white ants . . . they are all white ants . . .'

Choking on sobs, Otik bends down and observes thousands of white ants swarming around his feet and along the path.

* * *

4   An Ordinary Tale About Women and Other Stories

'Ma! Otik is crying in his sleep!'

Siti shouts to her mother in the kitchen, as she approaches Otik's sleeping area to retrieve a rag.

'He must be dreaming. Quick, wake him . . .'

Ma instructs the children to come to the kitchen to stir the rice to be served to the people helping to build the house.

Still sobbing, Otik comes to the kitchen, where Ma and Kak Umi are cooking rice and side dishes.

'What's the matter, Tik?' asks Kak Umi, smiling.

'Well, there you go . . . last night you were so spooked by the scent of pulai flowers . . . seems like a forest nymph came to sit on you, did it, Tik?' chimes Ma.

Still glum, Si Otik sits with legs dangling over the threshold of the door, wiping his nose with a sarong.

'Tik was dreaming . . .'

'What did you dream about, Tik?' asks Kak Umi, still amused.

'Our house shattered . . .'

'Then what?'

'All the people turned into white ants . . .'

Kak Umi, Ma, and Siti laugh till they tear upon hearing Little Otik's dream.

'You'd better quickly have your bath, Otik. If not, it won't be other people turning into white ants, it will just be you . . .'

Ma gets up to place a pot of kembung fish stew on the stove burner, moulded from still-wet red earth. On the ground, four or five people are whittling bamboo to make

At the Edge of a River

pelupuh cladding for the outer walls, planing wood for the room walls, splitting bamboo for the floor of the courtyard.

'We need to plant a few clusters of bamboo on that riverbank over there. If we don't, when the flood comes this year, it will erode by four–five feet.'

Everyone turns momentarily to gaze at the riverbank that Cek was talking about.

'This place will erode eventually. You shouldn't have chosen this area to build a house . . .' says Pakcik Yusof.

'This was the only place the Tok Penghulu, the village head, said was suitable. The rest of the land upstream and downstream belongs to other people,' Cek explains.

'This place is fine. Your children won't have to go far to collect water. The river is nearby. When it floods, you can use my well,' says Pak Yusof. 'My well is on high ground, the water that flows there isn't murky.'

'If it weren't for the kids, I wouldn't choose to live at the edge of this river, Pakcik. Their mother would prefer to rent a small house in Kota Bharu, there's one at Jalan Hilir Kota.'

'If it were just both of you, you could do that. When you have kids, how can you . . . everything there needs to be bought or paid for. Schools in the city are a hassle too. Here, if you don't have textbooks, it's not a problem, the teachers don't scold you or force you to buy them. If your clothes are shabby, you aren't forced to buy new ones. Even if you're an hour late, the teachers don't say anything,' remarks Pakcik Yusof.

6   An Ordinary Tale About Women and Other Stories

'Who's to say . . . the teachers themselves arrive at 8 o'clock . . . the morning ferry comes at 7.30, what time do we even cross the river?' adds Pakcik Daud.

'That's why I want to live in the village, Pakcik Daud,' says Cek, 'so that my children will be tough. Not like the pampered kids of Kota Bharu, dependent on their parents for this and that. In the village, during planting season, they can help uproot seedlings; during harvest season, they can help reap the paddy; we can buy a calf or two, and after school, the kids can take them to graze. If their folks can't prepare all the trenches to grow potatoes, they can help us to loosen the soil . . . isn't that right?'

'That's the way it is . . .' replies Pak Daud, 'if everyone just looks at Kota Bharu, Pasir Pekan will remain like this down to our great-grandchildren and future descendants . . . if one lives near the main roads, at least we can see the secondary school, passing cars, streetlamps on moonless nights . . . but tucked away at the edge of the river, what can we see?'

'What else do you want to see . . . your own children!' retorts Pak Yusof.

'We don't have any property,' says Cek. 'What can we leave behind when we pass away . . . just our children. Rich people leave behind property, great people leave behind their name, people like me only leave behind Little Siti, Little Umi, and Little Otik!'

'That's wealth too,' says Wan Derasid. 'That's what survives for generations.'

At the Edge of a River 7

'The two of you,' Pak Daud remarks, 'we told you to plan your family, but you want to have so many children as your legacy!'

'If we plan,' replies Cek, 'do you think in two or three generations our children will be like this? Don't hope for it, we'll be like mice in the water!'

'What do you mean?' asks Wan Derasid.

'Our line will be nearly extinct!' says Cek.

Everyone bursts into laughter at Cek's words. And the bamboo for the pelupuh walls is placed in piles to be woven by the community. After the meal, they will be immediately installed along the wet kitchen, the courtyard, and the rooms along the verandah. The staircase has already been installed by Wan Derasid.

Little Otik and Siti go back and forth from the river to collect water. Cek and the other men hear the children exclaim in delight that they no longer have to collect water from the well.

'When school opens next year, he'll be in standard one!' Cek announces to everyone as he sees Little Otik waddling along behind Siti, carrying a plastic bucket the colour of ripe betelnut.

'He's the same age as my Melah at home,' says Mat Noh.

Just then Ma calls Cek into the house to fetch beverages chilled with ice for all those helping to build the house. Cek returns with a blue plastic jug filled with a sweet green drink, flavoured with pandan leaves. They all rest for a

8 An Ordinary Tale About Women and Other Stories

while on the ledge, each savouring a glass of the refreshing drink. Pakcik Yusof sits on the ground facing the path behind the house.

'Who's that coming this way?' says Pakcik Yusof, looking down the path.

Craning their necks, everyone searches in the direction of Pakcik Yusof's gaze.

A group of four men is approaching.

'Who is it, then?' Pak Daud asks, wrinkling his brow as he tries to make out their identity.

'The one wearing the chequered pelikat sarong, white shirt, and yellow semutar is the Tok Penghulu,' says Cek. 'The one wearing grey trousers and a blue shirt is Mat Diah, I think . . . the other two I don't know . . . but why are they here?'

Everyone puts away their empty glasses and stands up. They dust themselves off—some with their hands, others with their semutar cloth.

'Ah, Tok Penghulu, please come in . . .' says Pakcik Yusof, bowing slightly.

The Tok Penghulu's expression is solemn, but he nods and smiles at all those present. The men come up to greet him, extending their hands in salaam. Cek walks to the stairs of the kitchen and asks Ma to prepare a drink for the important guest.

The Tok Penghulu beckons Pakcik Yusof to the side, away from the others. When Cek returns, the Tok Penghulu beckons Cek to join them.

At the Edge of a River

As Cek approaches, Pakcik Yusof casts his gaze to the ground and tries to watch Cek from the corner of his eye for a few moments.

'Ceksu . . .' the Tok Penghulu almost whispers, 'I have brought the representatives of the Tok Wakil here . . . they have a letter for you from the Tok Wakil.'

'What letter?' Cek turns to look at the other three guests.

'It's like this,' says Mat Diah, 'these two gentlemen are representatives of the Tok Wakil from the city. He wants to inform you that you cannot build your house on this land here. It's dangerous. When the flood comes, your house will fall into the river . . .'

Mat Diah glances at the Tok Penghulu and the two men accompanying him. They all nod their heads at Cek.

'But I can plant bamboo along the riverbank. If there's bamboo, the bank surely won't be eroded by the river!' Cek retorts. 'Look at the far end of the riverbank, aren't there three or four houses there already? Even closer to the edge of the river than mine. Isn't that more dangerous?'

'Those houses, too, will soon be issued a notice to relocate,' says one of the unknown men.

'It's all right, Sir. If the flood comes, I think I'll be able to handle it . . .' says Cek.

'It's an order!' exclaims Mat Diah. 'If you wish to comply, do so. If you don't comply, you will surely be fined or experience something unpleasant.'

10 An Ordinary Tale About Women and Other Stories

'But the Tok Penghulu gave me permission to build my house here before I relocated my house to his land the other day!' protested Cek. 'Why are you now saying I can't build here? After my house is almost complete?'

'That's what I said before, Ceksu, but these men are more powerful than I am. You can see for yourself . . .'

Cek starts fiddling with the axe tucked into the waist of his sarong, which he was using to split pelupuh bamboo. Pakcik Yusof comes up to Cek and whispers to him. As the Tok Penghulu and the others take their leave, Mat Diah turns towards Cek and smirks at him twice.

'That Mat Diah,' says Cek, 'I think he's the cause of all this trouble. He told me to put up the symbol of the water jug during the recent elections. I didn't care, I supported an independent party instead. He's already bullied me a few times. This time, he wins again. Damn it!'

'Enough. What do we do now?' asks Pakcik Daud.

'We still have a lot of bamboo,' says Pakcik Yusof. 'Why don't we build a raft house near my place over there? If anyone drives you out, you can drift away until you reach the estuary. The sea is vast, you can find a place to live anywhere . . .'

Pakcik Yusof takes Cek by the hand. The others are bewildered. From the house, Ma calls everyone to come in for their meal.

'It's torture,' Cek tells Ma in the kitchen, 'we can't build on *wakaf* land that belongs to God. But this is land that belongs to people. Yet there are those who are spiteful and hostile.'

At the Edge of a River

'That's the thing,' replies Ma. 'I already said it, Mat Diah can do whatever he likes. He told you to support his party, but you didn't, you supported an independent party . . . I don't think he's worried that we'll fall into the river when it floods. He doesn't want people who support other parties in this village.'

'What party is Pakcik Yusof?' asks Cek. 'And what about Pakcik Daud?'

'They're clever, not so blatant like you. You openly show that you hate his party!'

Night falls. Si Otik buries his head in his mother's belly again, unsettled by the heady scent of pulai flowers. Tomorrow, the day after tomorrow, or the day after, the little sibling in his mother's belly would be born on a raft house by Pakcik Yusof's place, or in an estuary, or on the open sea. Cek says Otik will get a dozen and a half siblings. He says with so many children, it's easy to form your own football team or *silat* team or whatever team you want, there's no need to combine with other families.

And Si Otik dreams he's playing with his chubby little siblings, all sitting in a row like plastic dolls. And the sickly-sweet pulai flowers fall to the ground, scattering ashen green petals around them like a soft carpet.

An Ordinary Tale About Women

This is just an ordinary tale about women. It's a short, uncomplicated story. In certain parts of this country, development is still lacking, and people lead simple lives. They strive to maintain this modest standard of living indefinitely through hard work.

Hence, there are squatter areas in this country where the people possess a strong work ethic to compensate for a life made despondent and desperate by the whims of fate and chance.

Yet, chance seldom sides with these people. Some husbands grow weary of such a life. So, they abandon their wives and children and marry other women. In Kampong Permatang Pasir alone, four such cases have occurred. To start, Abdul Rafar left his wife, Saniah, and their four children.

'I want to taste life in the city. You look after the house. The children aren't so hard to care for, they can even eat worms in stones,' he said to Saniah.

Abdul Rafar vanished for weeks on end, months, and then years. Saniah had to toil away to raise Jannatul,

14   An Ordinary Tale About Women and Other Stories

Adawiah, Taufiq, and Ridwan. Jannatul was forced to leave school at form three. The others were still in school—Adawiah in form one, Taufiq in standard five, and Ridwan in standard three.

When factory vacancies were broadcasted over the radio, seeking women between eighteen–thirty-five years of age and offering a salary of RM688 a month, with overtime pay, lodgings, and bus transport provided by the employer, Jannatul went to Penang to work in a factory. Every month, Jannatul returned to give her earnings to Saniah and the children. And so, their lives became a little brighter. End of story.

* * *

A year after Abdul Rafar's disappearance, Abdul Rashid, who lived at the far end of the village, was arguing with his wife, Mariani, one Wednesday evening.

'I divorce you with one talaq!' declared Abdul Rashid. 'Get out of this house. Take all your things.'

Their children—Zalifah, Zulkifla, Zulhan, Zanariah, and Zahira—sat huddled on the kitchen floor, all sobbing uncontrollably, except for Zahira who was still little. None of them fully understood what their parents were arguing about. They just knew that in recent weeks, their father often returned late at night. Sometimes when they were fast asleep, they were startled from their slumber by the engine of their father's Honda motorcycle pulling up in the driveway below the house.

An Ordinary Tale About Women

Usually this was followed by an intense argument between their parents. Sometimes they heard their father storm out of the house, rev up his engine, and ride off into the darkness. Their mother would be left there crying all night.

Mariani entered the kitchen, where her children were huddled. They saw Mariani's tears.

'Ma has to leave this house!' cried Mariani.

'Whoever wants to follow, come with me now,' she continued in a dejected tone.

Mariani took little Zahira from Zalifah's lap and walked out. The children got up and followed Mariani to the room to pack her things. They saw their father hurrying down the stairs to go who knows where. A moment later, they heard the motorcycle engine grunting fiercely and then it vanished.

Cradling Zahira, Mariani carried her bag and walked to the main road. Her children followed her, each carrying a bag filled with their clothes. While they were waiting for bus number 323, Abdul Rashid whizzed by on his motorcycle; he accelerated and threw them a contemptuous look.

Mariani told her parents in Kampong Aur Tujuh about her divorce from Abdul Rashid.

'I want to go work in a factory,' she told them.

'What about the children?' asked her mother.

'In two months, Zalifah will sit for her SRP exams. After that, she can look after her younger siblings . . .'

And so, every morning, Mariani borrowed her father's old bicycle to send Zalifah and Zulkifla to school, which

16   An Ordinary Tale About Women and Other Stories

was now far from their home. Then she would make a second trip, dropping Zulhan at school on her way to the factory. After school, her father would meet them and bring all three kids home on his bicycle.

After Zalifah completed her SRP exams, Mariani had to take her out of school to look after her younger siblings. Two years later, when factory vacancies were broadcast over the radio, seeking women operators and offering a salary of RM688 a month, with overtime pay, lodgings, and bus transport provided by the employer, Mariani sent Zalifah to work in a factory in Penang. End of story.

* * *

Around the same time, Abdul Jabal, newly retired from the Malaysian Armed Forces, returned to his home at the outskirts of a squatter area in Butterworth. After a couple of months of being with his wife Azizah and their children, his heart grew restless and weary. His wife's illness exasperated him.

What's more, his eldest son was already a young adult. He had not passed his SPM exams, he didn't have a job, he was just another mouth to feed. And who knew what would become of his second child. People say, with daughters, one should just marry them off quickly. After her SRP exams, perhaps, he could plan something for her. Two of his other children were in standard four and standard three, and another was not yet in school.

An Ordinary Tale About Women

Why didn't he realize all this while that these children would never bring him peace, especially now that he just wanted to enjoy his retirement? Why was there no improvement in his wife's condition of chronic fatigue? It seemed to him that he had been sacrificing himself for all these people. Yes, he had sacrificed too much for them. Now it was his turn to pay attention to himself.

Just three months after his retirement, Abdul Jabal left his house and rented another house a mile away. He took a second wife and opened a sundry shop with his pension and the bonus from his retirement.

At first, Azizah tried to reconcile herself to this new arrangement. At the end of the first month, she sent her eldest son Zahid and her daughter Wahidah to their father's house to ask for some money to pay the house rent and school expenses. Her children returned after a few moments.

'Papa chased us out with a *parang*, Ma!'

'How did that happen?' asked Azizah.

'When we came, Papa was selling cooked rice at his shop. We told him that Ma sent us to ask for money . . .' said Wahidah.

'Papa chased us out,' continued Zahid. 'He said we are no longer his children. If we go to him again asking for money, he'll strike us with his parang.'

By the fifth month, all of Azizah's children stopped going to school. They had been evicted by their landlord a month earlier because they couldn't pay rent. Now they lived

18 An Ordinary Tale About Women and Other Stories

in a garage next to a store that the owner had converted into a room for a rent of RM15 a month.

Azizah went to work at a nearby factory, but she soon had to stop due to frequent bouts of fatigue. They appealed to the village headman and the local Islamic Council for help.

'An unfaithful wife deserves such a fate,' some of them said.

The village headman and Islamic Council did not lift a finger to help Azizah, who wanted to claim alimony from her husband. Life seemed more and more suffocating. They barely managed to survive on what Zahid earned from washing cars. After some time, a group of Christian missionaries came to their rented room.

'We will assist with the schooling of all your children. Don't worry,' assured their leader. 'We'll bring you to a clinic. Don't worry, we'll cover the costs of your treatment.'

That evening, the missionaries brought three of Azizah's children to a shopping centre. They bought new school uniforms. They bought kitchen essentials to last a month. Then they brought Azizah to a clinic to treat her fatigue. When they sent her back home, they gave her money for three months' rent.

The activity of these missionaries soon fell under the suspicion of the Islamic Council.

'She's even willing to convert to Christianity, so long as they can eat,' remarked the village headman in disdain.

'What kind of human being is that?'

When Wahidah completed her SRP, Azizah sent her to work in a factory at Mak Mandin. After that, Azizah

An Ordinary Tale About Women

and her family no longer accepted aid from the Christian missionaries who tirelessly visited them. A while later, the Women's Crisis Bureau came to know about their situation. They were then moved to a more comfortable rented house and Azizah was provided with free medical treatment. End of story.

* * *

And so it was that Abdul Rahim, who lived at the outskirts of the Lubuk Tar squatter area, was one day fired from the factory he worked at for repeated instances of negligence. For months now, Jamilah had been the sole breadwinner for the family.

At first, he felt awkward living off his wife's blood, sweat, and tears, but after some time, Abdul Rahim felt at ease living like this. He had no desire to look for another job. In the morning, when Jamilah would leave for the health centre, Abdul Rahim would go to the neighbourhood coffee shop to chit-chat. He would sometimes come back for a while when Jamilah would steal a break to return home to cook. Then he would go out again to loiter and stroll around.

He was happy he no longer had to work. Day and night, morning and evening, his work would simply be rambling here and there to keep himself busy. Sometimes, he would spend hours at a rented bachelor pad, where young men would gather to watch porn videos.

Then, one night, while Jamilah was working a night shift, Abdul Rahim entered the room of Amalina, who was

20 An Ordinary Tale About Women and Other Stories

preparing to sit for her SPM exams in a couple of months. His body robust from the lack of work and exertion, his lust brimming from watching porn, he ravaged young Amalina till she was half dead.

'Don't tell a soul!' he threatened before he left the room. 'If you say a word, Papa will kill Ama.'

Amalina wept in inexpressible agony. Having gotten away with it the first time, Abdul Rahim took advantage of any chance he could until Jamilah noticed one day that Amalina's belly was bulging.

'Papa did this to Ama . . .' Amalina confided to her mother.

'Don't tell Papa, Ma . . . he will kill Ama.'

Jamilah felt all her strength leave her body. *What self-worth was left in the world!*

'Divorce me . . . please, leave this house,' Jamilah confronted Abdul Rahim. 'I pay the rent here,' she continued.

After Abdul Rahim left, Jamilah brought Amalina to her parent's house in Taiping. Leaving Amalina to the discretion of her parents, Jamilah returned home. She had two other daughters to care for—one in form four and another in form one.

'Let's go to the house of your Pak Andak in Lenggeng,' granny told Amalina. 'You can give birth there,' she decided.

And so, granny and her granddaughter took a night bus from Taiping to Lenggeng in Negeri Sembilan. As the express bus resumed its journey after a short stop in Kuala Lumpur, Amalina felt her belly twisting.

'Ama needs to go to the restroom, I need to poop,' she told granny.

An Ordinary Tale About Women 21

Most of the passengers in the bus were fast asleep. A little while later, Amalina returned to her seat. Granny was almost asleep.

'Done?' she asked Amalina.

'That thing fell into the toilet,' Amalina whispered to granny.

'What thing?'

'This . . .'

Amalina pointed to her belly. Granny sprang up and rushed to the restroom. Blood stains smeared the toilet bowl and the floor, as if someone had tried to wipe them away with tissue paper. And indeed, when flushed, the water in the toilet bowl did not go down. Granny hurried back to her seat and took out her face towel. She pulled off Amalina's underskirt and folded it together with the towel, wrapping it around Amalina's pelvic area to stem the bleeding.

It was still dark when they arrived in Lenggeng. They both got off the bus, but granny decided to not bring Amalina to her cousin Pak Andak's house. They changed their clothes in the public restroom at the bus stop, then took a taxi to Kuala Lumpur, then back home.

Amalina failed her SPM exams. To take care of her emotional state, Jamilah let Amalina return to Penang to work in a factory. End of story.

* * *

Here's a story that happened in the Angkasa Raya University of Malaysia. Many students there are single. There are first

22 An Ordinary Tale About Women and Other Stories

year, second year, third year, and fourth year students. Day after day, the students attend lectures and tutorials for this and that course. As is the case at other universities in Malaysia, UARM has more female than male students.

Because of this, many female students are worried that they will never have a boyfriend. This was what happened when a particular female student reached her fourth year and found herself still single. She then started showing interest in a male lecturer whose course she enrolled in three times.

Soon, they become a pair of lovers who walked here and there together, stirring up rumours on the UARM campus. In any case, this fourth-year student felt proud because her long wait had finally given her something she had never expected. To think she had bagged a lecturer, with the position of an associate professor and a big car, a Mercedes at that. A friend of hers approached her and offered some honest advice.

'Siti,' her friend said. 'He has a wife and four children! Imagine if you were in her place. Not like you don't know; his wife also works on campus. Find someone else . . . don't destroy someone's household!'

'What do I care!' Siti retorted. 'He has chosen me. It's up to him what he wants to do with his wife.'

'You'll have stepchildren.'

'Even better! I'll have *instant* children!'

It was later heard that the lecturer had divorced his wife with a single talaq. The wife was momentarily astonished at her sudden change of fate. A week later, she

An Ordinary Tale About Women

finished arranging the school transfers for her children. Then, without giving the standard three-months' notice, she resigned from UARM and took her children to Kuala Lumpur, where she started selling nasi lemak at a roadside stall owned by a close friend.

Now her children's academic performance has fallen from A to C. She no longer has time to help her children with their schoolwork. All her time is spent trying to make a living to support herself and her children. And sending them for tuition far away is not an option. She is simply grateful to God that her children never ask about their father. End of story.

* * *

And so it happened one day that several newspapers reported an incident of a UARM student who was charged in court for murdering her baby. Following this, the papers published reports of the discovery of the baby's body in the garbage disposal area near the Maju Mara Mall.

'Sungai Petani, 32nd August, a City Council worker found the corpse of a baby boy believed to be newborn in the garbage disposal area on Jalan Sang Kancil near here yesterday. The baby's body, with the umbilical cord still attached, was wrapped in newspaper and placed in a plastic bag.'

Accompanying the reports was a photograph of the accused student, handcuffed and head hanging low, being led away by police.

24 An Ordinary Tale About Women and Other Stories

'Hoooooiiiiiii!' exclaimed Mahfuz, a taxi driver casually acquainted with the family.

'This is the daughter of Cikgu Kassim, the senior assistant teacher of Datuk Saman Secondary School!' he told his friends at the taxi stand's coffee shop.

'I really know her . . . her mother is Cikgu Salina.'

'Oh, the one who drives the old blue Proton Perdana?' someone asked.

'Yes . . . the one whose house has a swimming pool,' replied Mahfuz.

'Are you sure?' asked another.

'I'm the one who sends the mother to school if the father has other things to attend to,' said Mahfuz.

'Look, her name is Salamanda binti Kassim! See, she comes from this state. Who else would it be?'

'Including this case, there are now five cases of girls dumping babies, killing babies,' remarks someone else.

'Why dump them? If they know how to make them, there's no need to throw them away! No need to kill them, if they gave one to me, I would take it!'

'Which five cases?'

'Didn't you read? Last month alone there were three cases. One who dumped a baby at a bus stop. Another who hung the baby's body on the fence of a mosque. Another who left a baby in the toilet of a bus . . . earlier this month there was one who threw the baby's corpse into a drain near the government offices.'

'I think,' said Mahfuz, 'in another twenty-four years, almost half the population of this country will be born out of wedlock.'

An Ordinary Tale About Women

'That's extreme!'

'What's so extreme about that?' asked Mahfuz.

'If ten people are born each day, a month is already three hundred, a year is already three thousand six hundred!'

Far and wide in every corner of the land, with the exception of a handful of close friends, nobody knew that some men were relieved to read the reports of the women criminals who had been caught for dumping and murdering their babies.

Zuraidin was taking a break at the factory where he works, talking about high powered motorbikes with Alimin and Meor Zainal, when someone came to tell him something.

'Jannatul has been arrested,' Danial whispered to Zuraidin.

'She's been accused of murdering her baby . . . that's surely yours, no?'

'Cis! Damn it, that's not my child . . . I wasn't the only one, you shared her too!' snapped Zuraidin.

'It wasn't just us, Zahid had her too,' said Danial.

Zuraidin knew that he was the first to approach Jannatul when she first started working at the factory. Then he passed her on to Danial. And Danial passed her on to Zahid. After that, who knows whom she was passed to. What they all remembered is that Jannatul asked them one by one if they would marry her. How stupid they would have been to accept her plea! End of story.

* * *

26   An Ordinary Tale About Women and Other Stories

Zamani was a dashing factory worker. With his fancy cruiser motorbike, he went around like the son of a wealthy man. He was often dressed to kill, in branded shirts, slacks, and shoes. He hardly ever smiled at the women factory workers. If Zamani smiled at a factory girl, she was considered lucky.

That's how it was when Zalifah, Mariani and Abdul Rashid's daughter, first came to work at the factory. At first, she thought Zamani was aloof and arrogant. But two days after Zalifah was declared as the runner-up New Year queen, Zamani coupled up with her. Which park did they not know on this pearl island? Which beach had they not set foot on? They knew them all, down to the secret crevices of rocks in Teluk Bahang, Batu Ferringhi, and elsewhere.

Soon, Zalifah's belly started to bulge. Zamani immediately stopped working at the factory and disappeared. In the end, Zalifah was sentenced to eight months in prison for murdering her baby and throwing it into a drain in Jeniang, Kedah.

Like Zamani, Khairul felt relieved and safe when he read about Salamanda being dragged to court for baby dumping. Now Khairul could focus on his final exams at UARM. Then he would get his degree and marry Dina.

That was how Abdul Mubin felt too, when he heard that Adawiah, the daughter of Azizah who suffered from chronic fatigue, was charged in court for murdering her baby and throwing it into the garbage at Jalan Lima.

An Ordinary Tale About Women

Rasuddin also heaved a sigh of relief when he read that Amalina, whom he used to bring around everywhere, had been arrested for abandoning her baby in a bush.

'All of this . . . ! It's all the women who are guilty!' says the *cecawi* bird to its family who had built a nest in a tree near the court. 'There's no male human being who is guilty.'

'Isn't that so . . .' chirped a little cecawi. 'It would be better if women had no sex organs . . . it seems that the men don't have sex organs, that's why they're all innocent.'

'Clever! Clever! Clever!!!' screeched the mother cecawi. 'Female humans are so clever now. They can make babies without men. Just like us cecawi . . . ha ha ha ha haiiiiiiii.'

The cecawi cackled so boisterously that the tree started to tremble. But nobody heard them because they are ghosts. The only ones who heard their voices and laughter were the walls, tables, doors, chairs, dust, and air inside the court.

A Letter to Mother in Kampong Pasir Pekan

Dearest beloved Mother,
most precious,
most cherished,
most revered Mother,

Forgive me. It's been so long since I wrote a long letter to you. I trust you are well and in Allah's care and protection. Insya-Allah.

Mother, I have received many letters from friends in the kampong, telling me about the huge storms that have been raging since the end of last year and have yet to subside. From their letters, it seems that these storms are even more violent than the great hurricane (I still remember your stories about the hurricane that occurred when granny was little. I can still imagine granduncle holding granny to take shelter under a straw covering as they lay in the sweet potato trenches in the middle of the field. And how, when morning had arrived and the hurricane came to rest,

30   An Ordinary Tale About Women and Other Stories

the entire kampong was left like a barren wasteland. And houses and trees were flattened to the level of the ground).

How is our house holding up now in the storms? In these circumstances, I feel it would be better if you come and stay with me, and don't return to the kampong. You will surely say that however terrible the condition is, it's still our home. That there will be no one to look after Cek's grave. There will be no one to feed our two or three ducks and chickens. And who will look after Bobo and Tampang and Tampang's offspring, they need to be fed too. I'm afraid that if there's a great storm, our house may collapse if it's struck by a stray coconut palm frond drifting through the air. If a branch of the durian tree snaps and falls, the bamboo wall we built by the river will crumble. And the bamboo fence we built around the well will surely fall apart if it's hit by falling branches. If the walls collapse, how will I bathe naked when I return to the village? You know well, Mama, that I like to bathe naked. Ah, how troublesome!

I'm worried that if the storms don't subside, the flood waters will rise. Our house will be in shambles. If it floods, our house will certainly drift away to the sea. I know, I should return to be with you, Mama, during this difficult time. I know that if our house collapses, it won't just be the structure that will be destroyed but the memories and legacy of our grandparents and ancestors will be lost, the earth that holds our blood, pus, piss, and poo will be washed away with the flood. And we will have no place left on land.

A Letter to Mother in Kampong Pasir Pekan   31

It seems that Mama should be prepared to face this great storm, as much as is possible on your own. I know that you don't find it difficult to live alone. I have always remembered you as a strong woman who worked hard to raise me and my sisters. Mama has done all kinds of work. So, I'm sure that you will easily prepare on your own.

There's just one thing that truly troubles me. Mek Yam, in her letter to me, said that bizarre things have been happening with these great storms, things that never happened during storms from previous years. I don't know how true Mek Yam's stories are. Mek Yam told me that a kind of dajjal comes flying in the eye of the storm, like the hairy caterpillars that are carried by the south-eastern wind in the seventh or eighth month. Mek Yam said these creatures are scattered everywhere. She herself came across dajjal mating in the earth near the ditch behind the kitchen while she turned the soil to find worms for the ducklings. Mek Yam said that she had never seen dajjal mating before that, but now she sees them often. At times, Mek Yam claimed, the dajjal are so bold that they mate at the banana tree bulbs in front of the house staircase.

Mek Yam has so many strange stories about these dajjal. She says that Mail discovered one rolled up beneath the seat cushion of his trishaw, ready to bite the backsides of his passengers. After that incident, Mail often finds dajjal hanging from the wheels of his trishaw when he pedals to Wakaf Bharu. Mek Yam says that Mail's wife saw dajjal gobbling up cooked food from the pots several

32   An Ordinary Tale About Women and Other Stories

times. Mail's father-in-law, too, came across a dajjal eating young green bananas in his orchard.

I also received a letter from Saudah, anxious and concerned about the affliction of these dajjal. According to Saudah, there are so many kinds of dajjal. And they breed so fast. She buried two dajjal that she found laying eggs in a sack of rice alive. And she cut down one dajjal father as it tried to crawl into the rice pot. She said she has killed so many little dajjal that hide in the coal pile, in bags of flour, in sacks of salt, even in the toilet holes. Saudah said that everyday her little boy Mamat catches dajjal with bamboo sticks and ties them to the trunk of the *rambai* tree behind the house. What's frustrating, said Saudah, is that these dajjal are so difficult to kill. Even after squashing two or three of them underfoot, till they turn red, they still don't die.

Worst of all is the letter I received from Peoh. She said that when she and Bedolah were about to make love in bed one night, she was shocked to discover a few dajjal spying on them from behind the door. Then, a few nights later, she caught a dajjal peeping at her as she was peeing below the house in the middle of the night. Peoh said the folks who live by the river are often disturbed by dajjal stealing their fish from the traps or intruding on women bathing in the river.

I am so worried about you, Mama. I'm afraid that the dajjal might enter the rice pot or sugar jar or gas barrels at home. What will happen if they enter our bellies? Even more frightening is the thought that these dajjal might

A Letter to Mother in Kampong Pasir Pekan   33

reach a stage where their skin grows so strong that they shape shift, like the hairy caterpillars of the south-eastern hemisphere that change into small white butterflies, flying here and there between the leaves and landing anywhere they please.

If it reaches this stage, how will we ever curb these dajjal, Mama?

I don't think it will be enough to kill off the mother and father dajjal. Because this kind of affliction is surely connected to an external power. We believe these dajjal are evil spirits, don't we, Mama? So, if you can conspire with the village folks, let's try to find the sites that have become dajjal centres of operation, where they mate and breed and procreate. Destroy those sites with hollow timber logs— lace the hollows with putrid sulphur so that the dajjal will be trapped in the logs and starve to death. Fill the buttress roots of large logs with poo. Tell all the kids to take a dump there, let the whole village stink to high heaven so that even dajjal won't want to live there.

If possible, at night, gather the folks in our neighbourhood to chant prayers to ask God to protect our kampong from the dajjal. Tell them that the dajjal pestilence is deadly, even more deadly than cholera. For now, the dajjal are just entering our rooms and spying on us while we sleep, gobbling our food, and taking our belongings. They might reach a point of such power when they devour all our hoes, parang machetes, klewang swords, and knives. It's possible that they will one day chomp off the heads of our villagers. I wouldn't be surprised if one day our own

34 An Ordinary Tale About Women and Other Stories

neighbours transform into dajjal, if they possess human bodies. How will we then be able to tell who is a dajjal and who is our neighbour? A situation like this is not at all unthinkable, for it has already happened in the past.

I suspect that the burning of dry rubber tree leaves some time ago was also the work of a dajjal—the fire reduced everyone's crops to ashes. Ah, Mama! I get so upset thinking about these dajjal. They run riot everywhere!

I also heard the news about the drama that was staged by the youth association of our kampong. I heard it was so good that it felt like real life. Esah Tuk Awang wrote to me about the drama and told me how intriguing the storyline was. The author is unknown. But, according to Esah, the drama revolves around the story of Mu'awiyah's battle against Saidina Ali. Esah said that many spectators who watched the drama were truly angry at the deceitful character of Mu'awiyah.

'Great Deceiver! Great Deceiver! Power crazy! Senile old fool! Even at this age you want to deceive people,' spectators heckled.

They shouted in protest when the forces of Saidina Ali could not defeat the forces of Mu'awiyah because they placed the Quran on their spears to fool Saidina Ali's men. Esah described how the audience threw rotten eggs and stones during the scene of Mu'awiyah's great deception. They were deeply upset when Saidina Ali was deceived by Mu'awiyah. It was Mu'awiyah who first challenged Saidina Ali to resign as Caliph. When a Caliph resigns, the challenger should also resign, so that the rightful leader

A Letter to Mother in Kampong Pasir Pekan   35

can be chosen through majority support. But Mu'awiyah's dishonourable men did not do this; when Saidina Ali resigned, they declared:

'We now pledge allegiance to the one Caliph, Mu'awiyah, because the other Caliph has resigned!'

Isn't it terrible, Mama, if this story is true? This is exactly the same as the dajjal!

This morning, I received another letter from Mek Yam. She said she has been asked by the youth association to play the heroine role in their upcoming drama. Mek Yam said she isn't ready yet. It's not just her who was invited to participate; the association invited all the kampong folk. Did they invite you to act too? Mek Yam said this drama has an episode about elections. So, they need many actors— young, old, male, female—to make it more realistic.

If they pay well, you should do it, Mama. It's good to earn something as an occasional stage actress. I'm just concerned that you may not be serious enough when you are acting. You may think it's just for fun. Don't take it too lightly, Mama, or they may think you don't know how to act. Do it seriously. If they ask you to do silat then show them some swift moves. If they ask you to dance then dance gracefully. If they ask you who you vote for then choose the person, not the tribe. If you choose the tribe, it may turn out to be a tribe who nominates a toad as their candidate. How tiresome, if our park is overrun by toads that go swimming in the lake, frolicking until they forget their wives and children at home, or until the locals around the lake get nauseous at the sight of so many toads.

36   An Ordinary Tale About Women and Other Stories

Play a little hard to get, Mama, to fetch a higher price or tell them to deposit piles of sand on the muddy path to our kampong!

Mama, here's a secret between us. Keep it safe and don't tell a soul. If others know, we shall be the ones who suffer. It's like this, Mama—I plan to go into some business. Go and find a few pairs, or as many as possible, of mother and father dajjal. Then, put them in a closed jar but not so tightly closed that they can't breathe. I plan to sell them to the national archive and museum. If we have a vast collection, I can sell them to zoos all around the world, too. Foreigners do not yet truly know the dajjal of our country. If we make a lot of money, we can build wooden walls and plank flooring, we won't have to live in a house made of bamboo. What's more, our kampong will achieve fame and glory if we export these dajjal overseas, for the local species of dajjal are indeed exceptional.

That's all from me for now, Mama. Take care of yourself in the great storms and be prepared for the flood that may occur if the storms continue like this. Keep the hearth burning with lots of firewood and coconut leaves and husk. If the flame goes out, it will be difficult to rekindle once the rain comes. Remember, Mama, don't let the dajjal creep into the rice pot and rice sack!

With salam and respect.

Your loving son,
Otik

The Scrawny Cat

Mahadi had been noticing the scrawny cat visiting his house for some time. He despised that animal. A patch on its back was furless, perhaps scalded with hot water by an unkind person or someone repulsed by its appearance.

The cat's face was marred by mange. Its patchy fur, once likely black and white, was now an indistinguishable dirty grey. Its bulging eyeballs, protruding from its bony head, made it even more unsightly.

During the day, the cat skulked beneath the houses, never daring to climb up. Only in the dead of night did it sneak inside. If the owners spotted it, they would chase and beat the cat until it was almost lifeless. Perhaps the cat understood how much its ugliness disgusted people.

Mahadi once saw the cat sleeping among the weeds near his house. He had the urge to beat it, even while it slept. But instead, he merely watched from afar, waiting for it to wake up.

Mahadi also thought of his pet cat, Si Puteh, who had gone missing some time ago. At first glance, the scrawny cat's spotted fur reminded him of Si Puteh. He had been

38   An Ordinary Tale About Women and Other Stories

playful and pampered, cute and chubby. Mahadi had tied a red thread around Si Puteh's neck to symbolically make him brave. He loved Si Puteh dearly, but one day, Si Puteh had not come home. Mahadi searched everywhere to no avail.

Days turned into months, and a year passed without Si Puteh's return. Eventually, Si Puteh faded from Mahadi's memory. He now had another cat named Chindai.

One day, the scrawny cat crept up to Mahadi's house, searching for scraps of food. There was a serving of stewed fish uncovered on the table. Although the cat was starving, it did not touch the fish. Perhaps it remembered the training of its former master: 'Food on a plate is not for a cat.' Perhaps the cat thought: 'No matter if one is ugly, so long as one is good.'

Mahadi heard the cat jumping in the kitchen. What was he waiting for! He ran into the kitchen, but the scrawny cat quickly leapt out the window. Mahadi impulsively chased the cat, throwing sticks and stones at it.

As Mahadi pursued the cat, he was stopped by Wak Dolah, a gentle old man. Wak Dolah scolded Mahadi for behaving so unkindly.

'Even though it's just an animal, we should look after it. Furthermore, if you kill that cat, it will die without sin. But on the Day of Judgement, you will carry its fur one strand at a time, each as large as a coconut palm, all the way up to the sky.'

These words struck fear into Mahadi's heart.

Chindai had just given birth to four kittens. Every night Mahadi would stay up to watch over them. A large black

The Scrawny Cat

tomcat was stalking the kittens, and Mahadi was afraid that the kittens would fall prey to it. He wasn't only worried about the tomcat; he was anxious about the scrawny cat too. If he could, he would have liked to kill both cats to protect the kittens from harm.

One night, as everyone was sound asleep, the black tomcat crept up to Mahadi's house and killed two of the kittens. The next day, another kitten was killed. Mahadi was devastated. Only one kitten remained. He seethed with anger at the thought of the two stray cats.

Mahadi devised a way to trap those wicked cats. He set up a snare made from jute netting at the opening through which the cats probably entered. Then he tied the snare tightly to a piece of wood.

As Mahadi was making the trap, he saw the scrawny cat eating one of his sparrows. He instantly forgot what Wak Dolah had said to him the other day. Slowly he crept up to the cat and hit it as hard as he could, striking the cat's leg. The poor cat ran away limping, leaving a trail of blood behind him.

A few nights passed and Mahadi's trap was still empty. The large tomcat did not come. At last, the scrawny cat came. As usual, it crept up to the house, looking for scraps of food.

Luck was not on the cat's side—little did it know that Mahadi lay in wait behind the door. With all his strength, Mahadi swung at it with a piece of wood, but the cat scampered away through a hole and escaped. Then Mahadi heard a terrible cry.

40   An Ordinary Tale About Women and Other Stories

Mahadi approached the trap he had set. His heart was pounding as he realized that his trap had caught its prey. The scrawny animal was writhing as it hung from the net. It howled so pitifully, as if pleading for mercy from a human being of conscience to release it from that deadly snare. Mahadi did not release it. He had gotten more than he bargained for, so he pummelled the cat to his heart's content.

After a while, Mahadi grew tired and left. The agonized cry of the scrawny cat grew weaker and weaker, until it disappeared completely. Only its body hung stiffly from the snare.

In the middle of the night, the tomcat crept into the house. Like a stroke of lightning, it seized Mahadi's last kitten. Mahadi woke up, but it was too late! The kitten had been killed like its three siblings.

The next day, Mahadi went to check his trap. With glee, he called out to his mother and father that his trap had caught its prey. But a shudder ran through his limbs when he saw the dead cat—its tongue dangling, its mouth agape, its eyes wild with a vacant stare. Sheathing his hands with paper, Mahadi unknotted the netting and the cat's corpse fell with a thud to the ground below the house.

Mahadi went down and dragged the corpse out. He grew pale, as if all his blood was draining from his body, when he caught sight of a tattered red thread amidst the frayed strings of the net. When he looked at it more closely, it became clear to Mahadi that the scrawny cat was none other than Si Puteh, his beloved lost pet.

The Scrawny Cat   41

Mahadi cried for his mother. She came without uttering a single word. They did not expect that Si Puteh would return after he had been missing for over a year. But he had returned in such a wretched state that they did not recognize him. He wasn't like before—cute and chubby, adored by everyone.

When he was ugly, everyone despised him. Wherever he went, he was chased away and beaten, which worsened his condition. Such is the fate of a mangy cat.

Overcome with regret, Mahadi slowly carried the corpse of the scrawny cat. *Stay here, Puteh, you died by my cruel hand*, Mahadi said in his heart as he filled the pit with earth.

For a moment, he looked at the *tembusu* tree that stood near the spot where he had buried the cat. Then, he gazed up at the sky and remembered Wak Dolah's words.

He felt the weight of each strand of fur, as large as a coconut palm, as he carried it up all the way to the sky. Then, he thought: 'What if I am punished just like the scrawny cat.' Oh! He seemed to see the shadow of the dead cat's head protruding out of the hole! As if it lay in wait to pounce at him. Mahadi ran back to the house in horror and dismay.

Spilled Rice

The wild banana leaves were strung. The *jering* beans were peeled. The jasmine and *champaka* flowers were threaded. Jarah had done it all. Only the banana leaves had yet to be stripped from their fronds. She didn't ask Bedolah to strip the leaves, fearing they would get torn or damaged.

'Bidah, you string the flowers! Bedolah, you pluck the jering stalks, carefully!'

The three of them went to work. They worked diligently, without saying a word. Jarah stripped the banana leaves one by one with her vegetable knife. The banana fronds piled up, each of them a new plaything for little Hani. Giggling with delight, she swung the fronds in all directions. She crawled around, then sat down again. Then she swished the fronds at Bedolah's back. Amused at his little sister's antics, Bedolah sometimes stood up to chase her. Hani laughed uncontrollably as her brother caught and tickled her. Mosquitoes buzzed around them with full bellies. Zabidah clapped one dead—she was quick to hunt down the wicked mosquitoes stealing her sister's blood.

There were already three tiny swellings on Hani's back. Pink like *jambu* blossoms.

After tearing the banana leaves off the fronds, Jarah folded them. A single fold into four parts. She arranged the folded leaves in a pile that reached her knees, tying them all together with a string made of dried banana frond. That task was done. If her mother asked, she would reply:

'This bundle has twenty pieces. And this one has fifteen.'

Her mother would say:

'Twenty pieces is one riyal. Fifteen is only seventy-five cents.'

Then, Jarah would count the jering beans, and tell her mother:

'There are five hundred beans in this basket. This one has two hundred. And this case has a hundred.'

And her mother would answer:

'Five hundred beans is only two and a half riyal. Five amas! Two hundred beans is only one riyal. A hundred beans is only one amas! If we earn four riyal, after dividing it into two for commissions, we keep two riyal!'

Then Jarah would count the jasmine and champaka flowers. Jarah would tell her mother:

'This tray has twenty bunches. And this tray another twenty. Forty altogether.'

And her mother would reply:

'Forty bunches is two riyal, if we sell them all. After dividing, we get one riyal!'

After that, the wild banana leaves would be carried up the stairs. The baskets filled with jering would be carried

Spilled Rice 45

up the stairs. The trays of jasmine and champaka would be carried up the stairs. Potatoes or vegetables would also be brought upstairs.

Mother would hold the woven *mengkuang* baskets above her head. Father would hang the rattan baskets filled with potatoes from a pole balanced on his shoulder. At times, the contents of the baskets would spill out during their journey. At times, they would spill on the bus ride. At times, while waiting for the bus at the roadside. And mother would carry those baskets home. And father would carry those trays and vessels home. At times, there would still be goods left in the baskets. At times, there would still be goods left in the trays.

Before leaving the house, mother would perform her daily tasks. Father, too, would attend to his daily tasks. First, mother would go to the kitchen. She would smudge her forefinger against a piece of coal, the black dust sticking to the lines on her finger. Then she would rub her teeth with the blackened finger. She would spit once, smear her finger again, continue rubbing, and spit again. Then she would wipe her forefinger on her sarong and tie her hair into a bun. Dusting off both her hands, she would call out:

'Jarah! Bring your little sister.'

'Bidah! Bring your little sister.'

If Jarah was holding Hani, she would bring her to their mother. If it was Zabidah, she would bring her. Mother would take the young child with both hands and place her on her lap. From the neckline of her faded kebaya, mother would bring out her breasts. And Hani would suckle to

46 An Ordinary Tale About Women and Other Stories

her heart's content. Hani's little feet would lift in joy as her chubby hands would grasp and pull her mother's nipples. Bedolah would come and say:

'Little Hani has no shame, suckling mama's tits! No shame! Woo woo!'

Hani wouldn't care. She'd suck and suck on her mother's nipples. When she had enough, Mother would say:

'Full already? Go, then, with your sister.'

Jarah and Zabidah would come to get Hani. Sometimes, Hani would whine, not wanting to be torn away from her mother's lap. Sometimes, she would cry, but only sometimes. Most of the time, she would laugh heartily.

Then Mother would instruct them:

'Jarah, cook the catfish as a curry with coconut milk. Add some *kandis* leaves. The dried fish should be grilled. Don't forget to bathe your little sister. If anyone asks, tell them I am in the garden. Tell them father is at the waterway. Close the door tightly. Watch the fire after you cook the rice. Douse it with water.'

Jarah would hear those instructions every day. Day after day, those same words, those same orders. Yet Jarah's heart neither grew weary nor was she angry or bored.

Father didn't say much before leaving. Maybe there was nothing to be said. But Father was a man of few words. Their whole lives, Jarah had never once been yelled at by Father, Zabidah had never been smacked, Bedolah had never been struck. And little Hani had never been subjected to harshness. Jarah had never heard Father complaining to Mother. She had only heard her father grumble when his potatoes fetched the lowest price. Or when the banana leaves were unsold. Or when the leftover jering beans shrunk and withered.

Today, Mother and Father went to the town early, leaving Jarah to look after her younger siblings. They had many things to sell. Banana leaves. Jering beans. *Chiku* and jambu fruits. Champaka and jasmine flowers. Such a day might only occur twice or three times in a month. Usually, just once!

Mother had already disappeared down the alley leading to the main road. Father had already disappeared among the weeds and thickets. Jarah sent Bedolah to bathe. She told Zabidah to take little Hani to the door sill. And she herself went about the task of killing the catfish in the earthen jar. She made sure they were properly dead. Then she measured two *ling* of raw rice in an aluminium pot. The water left from rinsing the rice was not thrown out; it was kept in a metal basin. This rice water is needed to soak the catfish so that its flesh does not give off a fishy odour. That's what Mother always told Jarah.

The rice pot was now on the stove. She blew at the embers till the flames were steady, her eyes red from the heat. Her fingers were smeared with ash and coal. While the rice was boiling, Jarah had to scrape the coconuts. Before scraping, the coconut needed to be husked. If there was a coconut sprout inside, it would be relished by Hani or Bedolah or Zabidah. She didn't need such treats. She was already a young adult of thirteen! She didn't need to eat coconut sprouts anymore!

48 An Ordinary Tale About Women and Other Stories

The morning sun blazed through the tree branches in the front courtyard of the house. Jarah had cooked the rice. The catfish curry was ready. The grilled fish was done. She had already tidied up the kitchen. In her heart, Jarah felt sympathy for her mother. Even if her mother didn't instruct her, even if her father didn't ask her, she would have done all these tasks willingly.

'Dolah, come here!'

Bedolah came, almost running. He thought it was time to eat!

'Help me carry these old *tikar* mats.'

'What for?'

'We are going to dry the paddy. Roll them up well, don't let them touch your skin, it will itch.'

Bedolah followed his sister's instructions with the careful attention of a child.

'Bidah, lock the front door. Come and help me tie the kitchen door. Bring the cloth that Ma uses to shade little Hani.'

Zabidah did as she was told. She reached for a piece of batik cloth that was hanging from a wire on the wall. She cradled Hani in one arm and latched the front door.

'Here, take this threshing basket, Bidah. Make sure it doesn't touch little Hani; her skin will itch.'

Jarah measured a small basket of paddy and dragged it to the doorway.

'Bidah, put Hani down. Help lift this basket onto my head.'

Zabidah put Hani down on the backyard floor. She carefully placed the basket upon Jarah's head.

Spilled Rice

'Alright, now carry Hani. Go down the steps carefully. Bedolah, you go first. Close the door tightly, Bidah. And cover Hani's head, it's hot outside!'

The three of them walked in single file. Bedolah was first, carrying the old tikar mats. Zabidah walked in the middle, holding the threshing baskets under her left arm and cradling Hani with her right arm. Jarah brought up the rear, balancing a basket of paddy on her head while clutching it with both her hands.

Suddenly, Bedolah cried out in joy.

'Aaaaaaaaaiiiiii.'

Jarah was startled. So was Zabidah. And little Hani too.

'Mushrooms! Mynah feet mushrooms! Look, there are so many here and there.'

Jarah glanced around to the left and right. Peering out among the dried leaves of rubber trees that carpeted the ground, were sprigs of striking vermillion. The intense colour didn't change like that of ripe betelnut on the earth among fallen leaves. These mushrooms had not yet bloomed. They were perfect for picking to make spicy vegetable stew.

'Let's go dry the paddy first. We'll pick them on the way back,' said Jarah. Zabidah and Bedolah followed her instructions.

When they arrived at the paddy field, Jarah told Zabidah to put Hani down. Zabidah plucked some banana leaves, laid them on the ground, and placed Hani on them. Bedolah rolled out the tikar mats. He was eager to get to work. The faster they worked, the faster they would be done, and the sooner they could pick the mynah feet mushrooms!

50   An Ordinary Tale About Women and Other Stories

Jarah poured the paddy from the basket onto the tikar. She strewed the paddy with her hands, so that the layer of grain was even and thin. If the layer was too thick, the paddy wouldn't dry thoroughly and would not be ready for pounding. Jarah's cheeks were flushed by the scorching sun. Her eyes watered. Beads of sweat dotted her brow and the back of her neck. Zabidah helped strew the paddy too. The sisters' hands grazed each other among the grains. Bedolah occupied himself playing with Hani.

Jarah wiped both her hands on her sarong. The paddy had been strewn. The heat of the sun would dry it all in just a few hours. They would collect it in the evening. Then the paddy would be pounded. Their mother would be happy. Their father would be pleased.

Jarah reached her hand out to Hani, who leapt towards her. In a single move, Hani was in Jarah's arms.

'Let's go pick the mushrooms, Kak?'

Bedolah couldn't wait any longer. He was afraid Jarah would forget about the mushrooms.

The three siblings walked home. Bedolah led the way, skipping. Zabidah walked fast, her hands grasping at the leaves that arched into the path. Jarah arranged the cloth that was covering Hani's head.

'Ha, quick! There they are!' Bedolah called in excitement.

'Dolah, take your sarong and make a sack for the mushrooms. Bidah, be careful, or you'll trample and crush them.'

They all started harvesting, hunched over their work. Even Hani plucked out one or two. Jarah was swift. So was

Zabidah. And Dolah too. In their hearts, they all whispered the same prayer—that no one else would walk by; that no one else would pick the mushrooms; that the mynah feet mushrooms would be theirs alone!

The mushrooms were now heaped in Dolah's sarong. Fresh and lovely. Zabidah and Bedolah carried one side of the sarong each, bearing their harvest of wild mushrooms. Jarah didn't allow them to tie it up in a sack, for fear they would get damaged. They might break or crumble. Bedolah was overjoyed. Zabidah was delighted. Jarah, too, was happy. Hani was fiddling with a mushroom that was somewhat wilted. She tore it up into tiny pieces, which she scattered along the path all the way home.

When they arrived home, they immediately set to work. Jarah peeled away the ends of the mushroom that were covered with earth. Zabidah looked out for caterpillars. Bedolah cleaned away leaves and other scraps.

'Bring me some paper,' said Jarah.

Zabidah went into the house to look for paper. She didn't find any.

'There isn't any, Kak! Where's the paper?'

Jarah was slightly annoyed. She got up without replying to Zabidah. Jarah felt around the shelf by the wall. She pulled out a tattered book. The book was of no use for anyone in the household—neither for herself nor Zabidah nor Bedolah. She had stopped going to school almost two years ago.

Jarah went out again, with Zabidah following behind her. Without saying a word, Jarah sat down and continued

52   An Ordinary Tale About Women and Other Stories

her work. Zabidah did the same. Soon, the dirt from the mynah feet mushrooms piled up on the paper.

It took a while for the mushrooms to be cleaned. But Jarah still had another important task to do: the mushrooms had to be cooked. She would fry them. Or she would cook them in a spicy stew, a dish that did not require oil. Hani could savour it. Zabidah could savour it. Mother and Father would savour it, too, when they returned home from the town.

Jarah cooked up all the mushrooms into a spicy vegetable stew. Bedolah's mouth watered as he caught a whiff of it. Bidah could almost taste its flavour. At times, Jarah could outdo her mother when she cooked vegetables and stews. Her father often said so. And Jarah felt proud of her skill.

Jarah scooped out the spicy mushroom stew into a small pot. She kept aside the first serving for her parents. It wouldn't be right for her parents to eat the leftovers of their children. Jarah then served the remainder of the stew in a large and deep dish. The four children would eat together. She placed the dish on the floor, steam rising from it in wispy puffs.

Zabidah immediately reached for the metal mug filled with water from the jar. Bedolah washed his hands in the backyard. Jarah had prepared three plates of rice around the steaming dish of spicy mushroom stew.

'Dolah, do you want some catfish curry with that?'

'No. I just want the mushrooms!'

'Bidah, do you want catfish curry?'

Spilled Rice 53

'No. I want mushrooms and dried fish!'

Bedolah couldn't wait any longer. He reached for the ladle resting in the mushroom stew and scooped a large pile onto the rice on his plate. Zabidah frowned, upset at him—she didn't want the entire dish of mushrooms to end up on Bedolah's plate. Hani flailed her arms, her small cries protesting Bedolah's behaviour.

Jarah refrained from serving herself. She had to resolve the commotion first.

'Dolah, take a little at a time. Or you won't even finish what's on your plate!'

Feeling that Jarah was on her side, Zabidah tried to grab the ladle from Bedolah's hand. Bedolah turned to evade her. Zabidah got up and reached over. Bedolah drew away his hand, tightly gripping the ladle. Bedolah whined. Zabidah whined. Hani thumped the bamboo floor.

'Hey!' snapped Jarah.

Startled, Zabidah accidentally leaned against Bedolah's plate, which slipped from his grasp. Half of the rice in his plate spilled onto the bamboo floor, falling through the cracks onto the ground below. A few chickens and ducks squawked as they scampered to pick at the rice.

Bedolah looked at his spilled rice in disbelief. He stood up before Jarah could seize him. He flung the ladle at Zabidah, striking her on the forehead. Zabidah started crying. Hani started yelling. Jarah seized Bedolah.

In a flash, Jarah's hands lashed Bedolah's ears. Her teeth clenched in fury as she glared at him. Bedolah started bawling. He kicked his plate, sending the remnants of his

54 An Ordinary Tale About Women and Other Stories

rice and mushroom stew flying all over the floor. Then Bedolah ran outside, stomping his feet loudly in frustration. Outside, he howled with all his might.

Jarah grumbled to Zabidah, but she didn't do anything. Zabidah was still sobbing. Hani was quiet.

With a coconut stalk broom, Jarah swept Bedolah's spilled rice and mushroom stew into the cracks of the floor. The chickens and ducks went wild below the house, as Bedolah's cries pierced the air. Jarah had no intention of inviting Bedolah back in to eat with them. She knew that he was not easily pacified. Eventually, he would stop crying on his own. Eventually, he would come inside and eat on his own. Or he would fall asleep somewhere.

The three sisters ate in silence. One mouthful for Jarah. One mouthful for Zabidah. One mouthful for Hani. The mynah feet mushroom stew was delicious. The grilled dried fish was tasty. Jarah was satisfied. Hani's belly was full.

After their meal, Jarah took Hani to the water jar to bathe her. She scrubbed Hani with a damp cloth.

Zabidah cleared the dishes. There was a little mushroom stew left for Bedolah. She added it to the portion they had kept aside for Mother and Father. Zabidah washed the plates then placed them on an old drying rack.

Jarah sat and cradled Hani to sleep. Little Hani was full and needed to sleep. Once she was asleep, Jarah would go and turn over the paddy they had left out to dry. Zabidah could watch over Hani at home.

'Kakkkk!'

Spilled Rice

Jarah heard Zabidah's voice like a croak from the kitchen.
'What is it, Bidah?'

There was no answer.

'Bidah?'

Jarah carried Hani and ran to the kitchen. They found Zabidah sprawled on the floor of the kitchen yard, still clutching a coconut broom, surrounded by a mess of vomit. Jarah put Hani down and immediately rubbed Zabidah's back. Zabidah retched again. She vomited non-stop, spewing all the rice and mushrooms she had eaten. Everything was mushed together. Jarah herself was starting to feel feverish and nauseous.

Zabidah kept throwing up, but now it was no longer rice and mushrooms—now she was vomiting blood! Zabidah's face was already turning a bruised blue. Jarah felt awful. Her own body was shaking—her throat was heating up; her chest and belly were bloating. Meanwhile, Zabidah was already fading.

Suddenly Hani started shrieking. Jarah didn't go to her immediately.

Leave Hani for a while. Let her yell there. She needed to help Zabidah. How could she help Zabidah? How could she stop Zabidah's retching? How?

'Ueekkk!'

Now Hani was throwing up. Jarah was delirious—chills were running down her entire body, making her tremble. She went to get Hani, who was still retching. Hani's face turned blue as her cries got stuck in her throat. Jarah

56   An Ordinary Tale About Women and Other Stories

started to cry. What kind of curse had befallen her sisters? Zabidah's body was limp like a rag. Hani's body, too, was limp!

'Kakkkk. . . water. . .'

Jarah turned towards Zabidah. Before she could get up, Hani spewed a downpour of blood onto Jarah's lap. Thick, dark blood!

'Maaa!'

Jarah screamed, as Hani's little body slumped in her lap.

'Kakk. . . water. . .' Jarah tried to get up to get water. Her sarong was soaked with Hani's vomit—full of undigested rice, full of undigested mushrooms, full of hot and thick blood. But she had to get up. She had to give Zabidah water.

Jarah's hand had not yet reached the water dipper. Her chest burning, she felt queasy and nauseous. Jarah threw up. Once. Twice. Three times. The fourth time, she fell into a squat; little Hani jerked in her lap. Jarah retched and retched. She felt all her energy drain away from her, till she couldn't move a finger. Her body was weak. Jarah's vomit splashed toward little Hani's head. The rice and mushrooms in her belly all spilled out. It spewed across the bamboo floor and seeped through the cracks. The chickens clucked in glee as they picked at it, and the ducks noisily wolfed it down.

'Maaa . . .'

Jarah's voice was breaking. Hani was curled in a limp heap. Zabidah had stopped asking for water. Jarah's body convulsed each time she threw up. It was no longer rice.

Spilled Rice 57

It was no longer mushroom stew. Now she was vomiting thick blood.

Jarah lay breathless on the bamboo floor. A patch of noon sunlight fell gently onto both Jarah and Hani's backs.

The sun was suspended in the west, casting a yellow shimmer on the trees of the village. Halimah walked first, balancing an empty mengkuang basket on her head. Samad followed behind her, a large rattan basket swinging from the pole he carried on his shoulders. Inside the rattan basket were kuih cakes for Jarah, kuih for Zabidah, kuih for Bedolah, and kuih for Hani.

Halimah heard Bedolah's wailing from afar. Samad, too, heard Bedolah crying. Halimah said to herself that her son had probably been pinched for being naughty. Samad said to himself that Jarah had probably twisted his ears for being naughty.

'Listen, Bedolah is crying!'

'He's a rascal. Jarah can't handle him.'

Halimah and Samad had almost arrived at the porch. They did not hear Jarah's voice gently cajoling Hani. They did not hear Zabidah talking. And they did not hear Hani laughing. The front door was closed tight and neat. Bedolah's cries grew louder and clearer.

'Jarah! Jarah!'

Stillness. Only Bedolah's cries echoed from the kitchen.

'Bedolah! Bedolah! Bedolah . . .'

Samad was now at the staircase to the kitchen. Two of his hens had keeled over near the bulbs of the banana trees.

58 An Ordinary Tale About Women and Other Stories

Samad was in shock. He probed the chicken carcasses with his feet.

'Bedolah! Open the door!'

Bedolah's cries went quiet. There was a sound of scuttling on the floor boards. Then the kitchen door opened. Samad went up. He was greeted by Bedolah's eyes, swollen from weeping.

'Mah!' Samad called out.

'Why did these chickens die?'

'Get up here quick, Mah. What disaster has struck!'

Halimah clambered up—her eyes wild, her brow furrowed.

'Jarah . . . Jarah!'

'Bidah . . . Bidah!'

'Hani . . . Hani!'

'Jarah! Bidah! Hani!'

In a manic state, Halimah touched the bodies that lay crumpled on the bamboo floor. Jarah's body was still warm, but her limbs were already stiff. Her clothes were covered in blood and vomit. Hani's body was just slightly warm, her naked body leaning against Jarah's belly. Zabidah's body was lukewarm, her clothes stained with splashes of half-dried blood and vomit.

Samad placed his ear on Jarah's chest. Jarah's chest was still, there was no rise and fall of breathing. He placed his ear on Zabidah's chest, which was also still, without movement. Then he bent down and placed his ear on Hani, whose body was now on Halimah's lap. Hani's chest was still, it did not rise and fall.

Spilled Rice

Halimah's tears now turned to howls. She sat cross-legged on the floor among the bodies of her three daughters. She could not believe that these three bodies were lifeless. She did not believe that their souls had left their bodies. One by one, she felt for the pulse of her daughters. But there was no pulse.

Samad carried Jarah to the living room. He carried Zabidah to the living room. Then he led Halimah, still cradling Hani, to the living room.

There were no tears in Samad's eyes. No sob emerged from his chest. No moan escaped his mouth.

Samad ran down from the house. First, he walked in the direction of Pak Cik Isa's house. Then he headed to Tuk Hassan's house. Then he went to see Pak Cik Par. He walked round and round the village for three miles to tell them what happened.

When Pak Cik Isa arrived, Halimah was still weeping. When Tuk Hassan came, she was still weeping. When Pak Cik Par reached the house, she was still weeping. This and that person came by, and Halimah's tears did not stop flowing.

Dusk fell. Halimah and Samad's house was lit by a bonfire of coconut husks and leaves.

Mak Cik Miah let out an incoherent cry in the dark as she stumbled on a duck carcass below the house.

Samad found that five of his ducks and drakes had died. Four of his hens had died. And thirteen chicks!

Samad searched for the old tikar mats that they used to cover the windows at night. He couldn't find them

60   An Ordinary Tale About Women and Other Stories

anywhere. Halimah was beyond any conversation at this point.

'Kak used those tikar mats to dry the paddy in the field,' said Bedolah.

Before Samad could ask Bedolah for details, he overheard Pak Cik Isa talking to Tuk Hassan.

'That grove of rubber trees had just been treated with weed poison!' said Pak Cik Isa.

'It's a good thing Bedolah's rice spilled . . .' replied Tuk Hassan.

And everyone looked at Bedolah, now soundly asleep at the side of the thatched wall of the living room, curled up with his rear facing the guests. Incense smoke gave off the scent of *kemenyan* benzoin and the sweetness of cut sugarcane wandered through the house, dousing the bodies of Jarah, Zabidah, and Hani in fragrance. The bodies were now arranged in a row in the centre of the hall, covered with Halimah's batik sarong and Samad's pelikat cloth.

A wisp of smoke slipped through a fissure in the window, left uncovered because the tikar mats were still in the paddy field. The smoke mingled with the gloomy night wind in the village that now felt empty and desolate.

The Dowry of Desire

When the time of puberty arrived, the Princess delighted in displaying herself in nature—free and open, caressed by a gentle mild breeze filled with the fragrance of buds blossoming towards the radiance of the sun. The Princess' breasts swelled with fresh curves as if they had been shaped by the hands of an accomplished sculptor. And her bum grew fuller and rounder as if moulded by a blacksmith with a sharp whittling knife. Her arms displayed a beautiful downy softness that roused the envy of all the leaves and flowers in the forbidden garden. Some bees and beetles fell mid-flight and flailed about helplessly on the grass upon seeing the Princess strolling in the forbidden garden without a thread on her body. Her silky fair skin quivered with each step as she skipped from one pavilion to another, through the red rose bushes and chrysanthemum shrubs and forty-day blossoms scattered in shades of white, mauve-grey, violet, blue, yellow, and maroon.

Dang Raya Rani, the head nanny of the palace, was at her wits end with the Princess' new antics. Whenever the Princess entered the forbidden garden to bask in the

62 An Ordinary Tale About Women and Other Stories

radiant morning and evening sun, Dang Raya Rani would trail after her, hunched over, along with seven lady's maids, each carrying an item of clothing that the Princess would have discarded from her body.

At midday, when the sun was at its zenith, the Princess went to bathe and swim in a pond filled with red roses that had been scattered by Dang Raya Rani and the entourage. While the Princess was bathing, Dang Raya Rani and the seven lady's maids were lingering patiently around the pond. Bearing a new set of robes for the Princess, in seven colours with seven kinds of flowers tucked into the folds, they sang pantun verses praising the beauty of the Princess from head to toe.

That's how it was until the Princess started her strange behaviour of stripping naked: Dang Raya Rani and the lady's maids could hardly handle her now. Nothing they did seemed right—if the ladies sang, it was all wrong; so too if they didn't sing. If they scattered flowers, it was wrong; so too if they didn't. At mealtimes, if Dang Raya Rani fed the Princess by hand, it was wrong; so too if she didn't. The Princess sulked and threw tantrums at everyone. Some mornings, Dang Raya Rani and the seven lady's maids would search high and low for the Princess, only to find her sitting on a white rock under a weeping fig tree, gazing below at the indigo mountain peaks in the distance. In those moments, only the Princess' lustrous ebony hair that hung down past her waist would be covering her bare breasts, back, and bum.

The seven lady's maids were fearful of the Princess' wrath that would strike them unawares. And, lately,

The Dowry of Desire 63

Dang Raya Rani had stopped asking them to prepare the Princess' robes, for the Princess simply refused to wear a single thread on her body. When sleep beckoned, the Princess would not want to be covered. She would only let Dang Raya Rani draw down the gauzy bed drapes, then she would lay on her back and fall asleep. No one could guess the cause of their beloved Princess' change in behaviour, except for Dang Raya Rani. One evening, the Princess asked Dang Raya Rani to accompany her on a walk in the forbidden garden.

'I want a magical flying horse . . .' said the Princess. 'Do you suppose my parents in the celestial realm will send me one?'

'Certainly, Your Highness. Make a wish to your parents, they are sure to feel it. But, if I may ask, where do you wish to go on that flying horse, Your Highness?'

'I am searching for something . . .'

'What is it you search for, Your Highness?'

'How would I know . . .'

Dang Raya Rani could only shake her head in bewilderment at the Princess' behaviour.

Late one night, Dang Raya Rani was woken up by the seven lady's maids with the alarming news that the Princess had vanished from her bedchamber. And Dang Raya Rani found that the flying horse was no longer in its silver stable. As dawn approached, the entire palace of the Princess was thrown into chaos. There was no trace of the Princess and no clue about where she had galloped off to on her flying horse in the dead of night. It was unlikely

64   An Ordinary Tale About Women and Other Stories

that the Princess had gone to the celestial realm to see her parents. Moreover, none of the Princess' robes had been touched, they were all still neatly arranged as before. The Princess would certainly not visit her parents in such a state of nakedness. As the first streaks of dawn vaguely appeared on the eastern horizon, at last Dang Raya Rani and the rest of the palace heard the tumultuous beating wings of the flying horse as it entered the palace gates. And there was the Princess, stark naked, astride her magnificent white steed. As she dismounted, her glossy black locks cascaded down her body, covering her breasts, torso, and back, all the way down to her buttocks. No one dared to ask the Princess where she had gone gallivanting all night on her flying horse. They simply watched as she left the stallion with the palace attendants to be returned to its silver stable, then went straight to her chambers and fell into a deep slumber.

The rulers of kingdoms across the Malay Archipelago, particularly those in the realm of the Gunung Ledang mountain range, were suddenly stricken by an outbreak of restless yearning. Their sleep began to be troubled by a beautiful and beguiling princess with an ambrosial fragrance, who appeared to them stark naked, riding a majestic cloud-white flying horse.

That is what happened on the thirteenth night of the waxing moon as Sang Betara, the King of Majapahit, was ruminating over the destiny of his empire. Deep in thought, both hands clasped behind him, the King walked out to the verandah of his *kraton*, bathed in the silver-white radiance of the moon. As he was reclining on his divan, crafted from black *chengal* wood gilded with gold lacquer, the King's mind wandered in a state of reverie. He felt as if he was being gently lulled by fairies in the sapphire blue sky. Suddenly, the King was startled out of his fantasies by an intoxicating fragrance that his senses had never before encountered. The King opened his eyes. The first thing he saw was the visage of a young woman of exquisite beauty. Her glistening body was half-concealed by her lustrous ebony locks, cascading over her ripe breasts and curvaceous thighs, as she sat astride a majestic stallion hovering in the sky with outspread wings. And the sparkle of her eyes was like a poison arrow, striking deep into the heart of Sang Betara until he fell to the floor. What an agonizing scene! The Princess gazed earnestly at the King, unblinking, as he crawled towards the silver fence of the verandah, where the Princess waited with her flying horse.

'Whoever you are, o fairy queen of the enchanted lands, take me with you to your realm, take me . . .'

The Princess smiled upon hearing Sang Betara's wistful plea, plunging him deeper into rapture and delirium. Tears ran down his cheeks and stained the floor of the kraton's verandah.

'Take me with you, I would go anywhere with you, I would gladly be your horse groom, o fairy queen, o magic stone, o potent jewel.'

The Princess was amused seeing Sang Betara, decrepit with age, especially around his eyes and mouth; she was amused too at how his broad nose seemed to spread over

66   An Ordinary Tale About Women and Other Stories

his round face. And so, the Princess pulled the reins of the winged stallion towards the full moon and slowly floated away from Sang Betara, who was left there hysterically pleading for her to not leave him. Gradually, the Princess merged with the silver-white radiance until Sang Betara could see nothing but the almost-round moon glowing softly. And Sang Betara collapsed next to the silver fence.

'There is a beautiful celestial princess casting her spells of love over these realms,' declared the court astrologer.

Sang Betara was driven to the brink of madness—night after night, the King would pace up and down the verandah of the kraton, awaiting the appearance of silver-white moonlight that would usher the beautiful princess, her naked flesh covered only by her lush black hair, riding her gallant white flying stallion.

Around the same time, when the orb of night was nearly in full splendour, the Sultan of Riau was savouring the pleasant night air on the verandah of his royal palace that faced the open sky. The refreshing air soon lulled the Sultan to sleep in his royal seat on the verandah. Just as she had visited Sang Betara, the Princess and her flying horse now appeared before the Sultan of Riau. In those brief moments of slumber, the Sultan of Riau saw a vision of the princess, heralded by silver-white moonlight, slowly approaching his palace amidst the relentless flurry of the beating wings of a flying horse. The Princess gazed at the Sultan with such melancholic longing that it pierced his heart and made him weep. At the sound of the Sultan's

The Dowry of Desire 67

first sob, the Princess spurred her steed and vanished into the night sky still shimmering with moonlight. For weeks on end, the Sultan of Riau seemed to be possessed by a wicked spirit—he could neither eat nor sleep and thought obsessively of the bewitching Princess who had appeared to him naked, covered only by her lustrous black locks, astride a magnificent, winged stallion. For weeks on end, the Sultan of Riau forgot and neglected his queen.

And it so happened on the thirteenth night of the waxing moon, that as the Raja of Lingga slept soundly beside his queen consort, he had a visitation by a princess of exquisite beauty, her glistening body utterly unclothed as she rode a majestic flying horse. On the following full moon night, the King of Terengganu dreamt that an ethereal princess came to him, stark naked, astride a white winged stallion hovering in the silver-white moonlight. When he tried to touch the Princess' outstretched fingers, she spurred her steed and they took to the sky, her long black tresses billowing like a sail behind her. The King of Terengganu fell into a state of disoriented frenzy—he could not eat or sleep until the most powerful *bomoh* in the kingdom was summoned and bathed him in the healing water of the seven springs.

For months on end, the rulers of kingdoms in the Malay Archipelago were plunged into delirious desire by the bewitching Princess. Except for Sang Betara, none of them revealed their visitations to anyone lest their queen consorts find out and accuse them of lovesick infatuation. So, they all tried to hide their lustful longing while secretly

68   An Ordinary Tale About Women and Other Stories

wishing that the Princess would appear again. But the Princess did not return.

And it so happened that one night, when a silver-white full moon illuminated the sky, Sultan Mahmud, the ruler of Malacca, was troubled by feelings of guilt and anxiety. The elder courtiers were urging him to take a queen consort to replace the departed mother of his son, Raja Ahmad. Although the bachelor's lifestyle he had been engaging in since the death of the queen was no reflection of his faithfulness or love towards her, the Sultan could not bring himself to choose a wife. In his eyes, no princess he had encountered from the kingdoms of the Malay Archipelago was worthy of becoming his queen. After all, Sultan Mahmud of Malacca was a ruler of true sovereignty, who traced his lineage to Nisruwan Adil, descendant of Alexander the Great, king of kings, king of the highest dignity and grace, the Almighty's representative on earth.

For the past few months, the Sultan had been contemplating who would be his new queen, to sit beside him on the throne of the sovereign kingdom of Malacca. As he was lost in thought that night, gazing at the resplendent full moon, he suddenly noticed a speck of light moving in the sky. It grew larger and brighter as it approached, and from it emerged a princess of exquisite beauty. Her naked body veiled only by her long, lustrous hair that covered her breasts and back, she rode a white stallion relentlessly beating its wings. As she drew near, an intoxicating fragrance flooded the Sultan's senses.

Sultan Mahmud stood up and walked to the edge of the palace verandah. The Princess was still there, observing

The Dowry of Desire 69

him with her gentle, alluring expression. Draped only by her tresses, her bare skin glistened in the limpid light of the moon.

Sultan Mahmud was stunned. As if under a spell, he forgot himself completely.

The Princess did not move an inch, her steed flapping its wings steadily as they hovered mid-air. Soon, tears of longing trickled from Sultan Mahmud's eyes.

'Come closer to me, o queen of the moon,' said Sultan Mahmud as he stretched his arms out towards the Princess. 'Come to me, I can't approach you any more than this— look: there is no bridge, this verandah ends here, come closer to me so that I may touch the lock of your hair.'

The Sultan was now weeping. The Princess slowly approached the fence of the palace verandah. The flying stallion alighted on the verandah and the Princess gracefully dismounted and stood before Sultan Mahmud.

No longer able to control himself, Sultan Mahmud flung himself at the Princess' feet. The Princess reached down and lifted the Sultan's chin then caressed his hair softly. Sultan Mahmud felt that moment to be infinitely more blissful than all the millions of nights that had preceded it.

'Who are you, my Princess?' asked Sultan Mahmud.

'I am Puteri Gunung Ledang,' replied the Princess.

'I wish to seek your hand in marriage and make you my queen. Would Your Highness accept my proposal?'

For the first time, the Princess smiled at Sultan Mahmud and nodded. Sultan Mahmud embraced the Princess' legs, then lifted her up. The Princess squirmed slightly, making Sultan Mahmud drunk with desire.

70   An Ordinary Tale About Women and Other Stories

'I shall come to see you again, Your Majesty,' said the Princess.

With great reluctance, Sultan Mahmud placed her onto the back of her flying horse. The Princess waved and smiled as she bid him farewell then took off like lightning on her steed and vanished into the silver-white moonlight. As soon as the Princess was out of his sight, Sultan Mahmud lost control of his thoughts and emotions. He summoned his elder courtiers for an audience with him in the middle of night. The royal astrologer advised that such proceedings would be inauspicious and that they should wait until the next day.

Sultan Mahmud could not sleep a wink all night. In his eyes, the Princess' alluring body—her delicate soft arms as fine as tapestry silk, her bountiful breasts, her eyes that sparkled with the lustre of pearls—was without equal in this world. Everything about her was so tantalizing that Sultan Mahmud imagined a million demigods kneeling at her lovely, fair, velvety feet. The ambrosial perfume that wafted from her body was far beyond any earthly aroma of flowers, amber, and musk. At daybreak, Sultan Mahmud was still inhaling his hands where they had touched the Princess' skin. It seemed to him that the halls of the palace were now filled with her intoxicating scent. He had never before savoured such a fragrance, at once sensual and sublime.

'Whatever the Princess commands, all you courtiers are to follow. I do not wish to have anyone but her as my queen.'

The Dowry of Desire

And so, the seasoned warrior and admiral, Laksamana Hang Tuah, ever loyal and dutiful and ready to serve the Sultan of Malacca, obeyed the Sultan's command to lead the royal delegation together with Sang Setia to seek the hand of Puteri Gunung Ledang. There were moments on their journey when Hang Tuah was left panting—the energy of his youth had given way to age. The delegation was forced to take breaks along the way to allow the elders Hang Tuah and Sang Setia to rest. All the indigenous people of the villages had been ordered by the village chiefs to help clear the path for the delegation. By the time they arrived at the foot of the mountain, Gunung Ledang, Hang Tuah and Sang Setia were so overcome with exhaustion that they could not continue the journey.

'It would be best for the elder statesmen to wait and rest here,' said Tun Mamat. 'Allow me to ascend the mountain. I request for two young and able-bodied companions who can climb against the wind.'

'Choose whoever you see fit, Sir' replied Hang Tuah, now breathless and weak. 'I am utterly disappointed that I cannot complete this task for His Majesty. If I were younger, I would certainly attend to it myself. If only human beings could fight the tide of time and the onset of old age!'

'Do not despair, Your Grace,' said Tun Mamat. 'You have served the Sultan of Malacca with such loyalty and courage for decades, that the younger courtiers have hardly had a chance to serve His Majesty at all. Please entrust me this time with this most serious task.'

72   An Ordinary Tale About Women and Other Stories

'Rest assured, you have my trust, Tun Mamat. Let us hope it is not too late to fulfil the Sultan's command.'

And so, Tun Mamat, accompanied by two agile men, made their way to the peak of Gunung Ledang. The higher they climbed, the stronger the wind blew against them. Tun Mamat felt as if all the trees on this sacred mountain were greeting their arrival. Stalks of enchanted bamboo gave out sweet cries of longing as the wind caressed them, so sweet that birds on a wing stopped to listen to their song. Leaves of unknown trees gently beckoned Tun Mamat and his men. The higher they climbed, the more wondrous the vistas that unfolded before them were. The morning mist encircling the mountain peak cast a shade of blue over the verdant jungle.

When the sun was almost directly overhead, Tun Mamat and his men finally reached the peak of Gunung Ledang. They were captivated by the breathtaking view that greeted them: a vast garden with grass like green velvet, where a myriad of flowers bloomed. Yellow, lilac-white, and red chrysanthemums, sunflowers, roses, and champaka adorned the shrubs and shady trees, filling the entire garden with their heady fragrance. Lining the paths, zinnia blossoms in vibrant colours basked in their fresh beauty. The chirping of birds resounded through the sprawling garden, while beetles, large and small, in shades of green, blue, black, and yellow flew among butterflies with iridescent wings. Tun Mamat and his men had never before encountered such natural splendour. Entering the garden cautiously, Tun Mamat made his way towards its

The Dowry of Desire

centre. There, he noticed a charming pavilion tiled with gleaming white marble, crafted from the most magical material. The pillars were made from bone and ivory, the attap roof was woven from hair, and the floor was made from bone. In front of the pavilion was a pond with crystalline blue water, where lotuses of pink, white, and crimson popped their heads above the surface between their large leafy pads.

The thoughts of Tun Mamat and his men were swarming in fantasy. They stood in a row facing the pavilion.

Sana sini gigi menimang,
Hendak makan ikan di dalam telaga;
Lagi lemak telur berlinang,
Sisiknya lekat pada dada.

Teeth grate against each other,
Craving the fresh fish in the well;
The riper the roe, the sweeter the flesh,
Its scales cleave closer to the breast.

Tun Mamat turned around upon hearing someone recite a pantun in a melodious voice. But no one was there—only a large white rose stood out against the leaves and flowers swaying their stalks in the breeze.

Dang Nila memangku puan,
Berembang buah pedada;
Adakah gila bagimu tuan,
Burung terbang dipipiskan lada.

74   An Ordinary Tale About Women and Other Stories

> Dang Nila placed in the betel box,
> The berembang and pedada fruit,
> Desire makes a fool of you, Sir,
> The bird escapes while you grind the pepper.

Again, Tun Mamat and his men were startled by a sweet voice that seemed to come from above the blue *tanjung* flower tree.

'Who is singing that pantun?'

'No idea,' his two men said in unison.

'It's us, of course!' replied the white rose and blue tanjung flower.

Just then, Tun Mamat realized that there was a figure sitting above the pavilion. An elderly woman with pure and radiant features was seated with her legs folded, attended to by four beautiful maidens. They were clad in glistening pale-yellow sarongs, with maroon velvet shawls draped over their bare shoulders. When the elderly woman cast her gaze at Tun Mamat, he could feel the lure of the light in her eyes soften all his limbs.

'Where have you come from? What is your name?' asked the elderly woman.

'I am Tun Mamat, and these are my men. I have come at the command of my master, the Sultan of Malacca, Sultan Mahmud Shah.'

'For what purpose?'

'To seek the hand of the Princess of Gunung Ledang. The Lord Admiral and Sang Setia are waiting at the foot of

The Dowry of Desire

the mountain, they have not enough strength for the climb. What is your name, My Lady?'

'I am Dang Raya Rani, and these are the lady's maids of the palace. I am the nanny of the Princess of Gunung Ledang. If the Sultan Malacca's intent is true, allow me to excuse myself to convey this message to the Princess.'

With that, the old woman and the four maidens vanished into thin air. And the pavilion stood empty and vacant. For a few moments, Tun Mamat and his men heard a murmur, *hm . . . hm . . . hm . . .* sung sweetly by a chorus of voices that seemed to come from nowhere. At times, the tone was so lilting and melancholic that it pierced Tun Mamat's heart. At times, the chorus soared up in melodic peals. Tun Mamat and his men had never before heard such ethereal voices—it was impossible to compare the sweetness of the chorus to any music of the world. Tun Mamat and his men were enraptured, lost in fantasy as if cradled by delightful dreams.

Adrift in a sea of bliss, Tun Mamat and his men saw a group of beautiful and alluring maidens approaching the pavilion from afar, singing and laughing. They were clad in gauzy soft drapes, iridescent with the seven colours of a rainbow. Swaying gracefully as they walked, their lithe bodies moved like ballerina dolls on the palm of a hand.

'My lord,' one of the maidens called out. 'Is it true that you have come on behalf of your king, to seek the hand of our queen?'

'It is true,' replied Tun Mamat.

'Is your king a human being or is he a fairy nymph like us?' asked another.

'No, our king is a human being,' replied Tun Mamat.

'If he is human, surely he is higher in rank and honour than us,' retorted the first. 'Why does your king wish to wed our queen, who is not of his kind?'

'Our king wishes to be the most distinguished of all the kings of this realm. If he was to wed the princess of an ordinary king, he would be no different than all the other kings of this realm.'

'Is that true?' exclaimed another maiden. 'His king wishes to elevate his honour, by marrying a fairy princess . . .'

'Yes.'

'What kind of honour would he attain, if your king weds a fairy nymph, a mere lowly creature cursed by God? Is he truly willing to do this?'

'He is certainly willing.'

'To lower his own dignity in order to distinguish himself with a rare privilege?'

'Yes.'

'O fellow fairies! O trees! O clouds, O sky, O sun, O wind, O breeze! Hark, take heed! The King of Malacca who professes to be Allah's representative on earth, wishes to find, among all the noble creations of God, something so exquisite and glorious, that he seeks a fairy as a bride! Isn't it amusing?'

'It is surely amusing!' resounded the fairies in reply.

'Laugh then, if it's amusing! Ha ha ha ha!'

The Dowry of Desire

'Ha ha ha ha!'

Tun Mamat and his men felt their hair stand on end at the eerie, shrill laughter of the fairies that echoed continuously over the peak of Gunung Ledang.

'You should tell your king that he would be better off choosing a female goat or cow rather than a fairy as a bride! Those two beasts are more noble creatures in the eyes of God!'

Furious at the insult of the fairies, Tun Mamat drew his *keris* dagger and was ready to strike it deep into their ribs. Just then, an old hunchbacked woman with long white hair that hung all the way to the ground approached the pavilion, surrounded by a flock of beautiful fairies. Tun Mamat gazed at the crone's face—it was wrinkled and wizened but a gentle and pure light shone from her eyes. He returned his keris to its sheath. As the old woman approached, all the fairies stood aside to make way for her, bowing their heads in deference and loyalty. The crone stopped in the middle of the pavilion and looked in Tun Mamat's direction. Her glossy white tresses cascaded down her breasts and covered the floor of the pavilion.

'My lord,' said the old crone, 'the Princess commands, if the Raja of Malacca truly wishes to make her his bride, he must offer a dowry of seven trays filled with the hearts of mosquitoes, seven trays filled with the hearts of germs, a barrel of tears, a barrel of young betel nut juice, a bowl of the king's blood, a bowl of the blood of his prince named Raja Ahmad. To ease his journey, the Raja of Malacca must build a golden bridge and a silver bridge from his palace

78   An Ordinary Tale About Women and Other Stories

to the peak of Gunung Ledang. If all these conditions are met, His Majesty's wish will be fulfilled.'

As soon as she had uttered those words, the old hunchbacked woman vanished from sight.

'*Tak tak tumm!*' The fairies chortled with laughter. 'There you go, that's the dowry of the lovely fairy Princess who can raise the honour of the King of Malacca! *Tak tak tumm!* Ha ha haiiii!'

Tun Mamat had no strength left to remain at the pavilion listening to the taunts of the fairies. He signalled to his men to start their descent. The whole flock of fairies followed at their heels.

'Remember, my lord,' they chimed, 'once the golden bridge and silver bridge are complete, the King of Malacca should station five thousand brave and reliable soldiers to stand guard. Who knows, the bridges may fall prey to bandits or a rival king! Then the King of Malacca and his princess would never set foot on it! Ha ha haiiii! Ha ha haiiii!'

Eventually, the fairies let Tun Mamat and his men descend from the peak of Gunung Ledang.

'Farewell, loyal servants!' they called out.

The fairies then gathered again in the garden pavilion.

'The people of Malacca are damned!' the fairies moaned. 'They will all be forced to weep without end for no reason, just to harvest their tears for their king. Who knows how long they will need to weep.'

'They will weep until they die! It won't just be enough tears to fill seven barrels. They will weep over their gold

The Dowry of Desire

and silver confiscated by their king. They will weep over the faeces and urine and vomit that they are forced to present in brass trays to the king, so that countless germs may fester for them to collect their hearts. Seven trays, not seven jasmine petals! Just think, how long the people of Malacca will have diarrhoea to provide an endless supply of cholera germs! And what's worse, the mosquitoes will diminish dramatically since they will be killed for their hearts. We all know that mosquitoes help to breed germs in human bodies. Ah, the people of Malacca are truly damned at this time!'

'The Sultan of Malacca will surely feast ten times a day with his son!' exclaimed one of the fairies. 'If not, how would he collect a bowl of blood from his prince? He'll be a fat king, and his prince will be as chubby as a piglet!'

'Ah, it's just one bowl! If I were the Princess, I would have demanded seven bowls of blood! It's easy to fill a bowl—if the king suffers from constipation and piles, even that blood would soon fill a bowl!'

Dead silence filled the royal hall of Sultan Mahmud's palace. Everyone bowed their heads towards the floor and didn't dare look up. The Sultan of Malacca was sullenly contemplating the bowl that was to be filled with blood drawn from his body and another bowl to be filled with blood from the body of his son. What agony it would be to draw that much blood from a king and his prince! Utter agony!

'I do not care about the seven barrels of tears, the golden bridge, the silver bridge, and all the rest. The people

80   An Ordinary Tale About Women and Other Stories

of Malacca are many, there's nothing we can't do. . . it's only the blood that is difficult. Nevertheless, Grand Vizier and all you noblemen, you may begin assembling this dowry and constructing those bridges. I command it to be done. When it is done, it shall be presented to me. We will leave the blood for last.'

And so, for many years the people of Malacca were forbidden to do anything except fulfil the royal dowry— the women killed mosquitoes and looked for germs all day and wept their eyes out all night; while the men became rogues, bandits, robbers, pirates, and murderers from dawn to dusk and dusk to dawn in search of gold and silver. Famine and hunger soon spread throughout the kingdom of Malacca. Every day, corpses were scattered around the village huts and dirt paths. The stench of decaying flesh permeated the villages and crept all the way to the paddy fields overgrown with sedges and rushes. Animals dropped dead like flies and plants wilted, suffocated by the putrid air. The villagers lost their appetite and could not eat in the midst of this stink, until they were nothing but skin and bones.

One day, as dusk was approaching, the Grand Vizier sought an audience with Sultan Mahmud in the palace.

'We have collected enough germ hearts to fill seven trays, Your Majesty. If Your Majesty commands us to fill ten trays, we shall fulfil your command.'

'What about the rest?'

'The mosquito hearts are ready, seven trays in all. We have seven barrels full of young betel nut juice and seven

The Dowry of Desire

barrels brimming with tears. The villagers across the river and upstream have cut down all their betel nut trees.'

'The bridges?'

The Grand Vizier fell silent and gazed down at his lap.

'Forgive me, Your Majesty, there is not enough material . . .'

'Did I not command that all the gold and silver in the kingdom's treasury be put to use?'

'Forgive me, Your Majesty, the builders say that all that gold and silver is only enough to build one or two pillars of a bridge. To build a bridge from Malacca to Gunung Ledang, we would need gold and silver as vast as the hill behind the royal palace!'

Sultan Mahmud rose from this throne in a state of rage.

'You insult me, Mamak Bendahara! Take all the gold and silver in the treasury, and whatever gold and silver exists anywhere in the kingdom! Order the men of Malacca to become pirates and bandits!'

'Forgive me, Your Majesty. If that is Your Majesty's command, I shall make arrangements for the ceremony to lay the foundation of gold and silver after *malam tujuh likur*, the night of power in the final days of Ramadan . . .'

'Why wait till then? Why should we wait for malam tujuh likur, why can't we perform the ceremony on any other night?'

'We can, Your Majesty, but on malam tujuh likur there is no moon, our enemies will not see us building the bridge.

An Ordinary Tale About Women and Other Stories

If there is a moon, the gold and silver pillars will surely shine bright . . .'

'Do it at your discretion, then, I shall simply attend . . .'

'Very well, Your Majesty!'

When the anticipated night of malam tujuh likur arrived, Sultan Mahmud's procession made its way from the palace compound to the city gates for the ceremony to lay the foundation of the golden and silver bridges from the Malacca Palace to Gunung Ledang. No less than fifty elephants accompanied the royal procession, all decorated with tassels and beads, bearing howdahs in various colours according to the rank of the respective nobles. Heralds and guards carrying ceremonial spears marched in rows to the right and left of the elephants. The beating of gendang drums resounded through the air. The night was ablaze with palm-leaf torches that illuminated Sultan Mahmud's procession.

Duuuuuuuummmmmm! Duuuuuuuummmmmm! Dummmm mmmmm!

Suddenly the entire city of Malacca shook. The procession stopped in its tracks.

Dummmmmm! Dummmmmmmmmm! Duuuuu! Dummmmm!

Noisy gunfire and explosions rocked the city. People ran helter-skelter, screaming and disoriented.

'The White Bengalis are firing at Malacca! The White Bengalis are shooting! The shores of Malacca are under attack!'

'Retreat to the palace!' commanded Sultan Mahmud.

The Dowry of Desire 83

The courtiers and guards were in a state of panic and chaos. All the gold and silver that had been piled up for the ceremony to lay the foundations of the bridges was now strewn and scattered and stamped underfoot by elephants, horses, and natives running aimlessly for their lives.

Inside the palace—the trays of mosquito hearts, trays of germ hearts, barrels of young betel nut juice, and barrels of tears were violently tossed and shattered, struck by pillars and pieces of wood blown apart by cannon fire. All the fine royal tapestries, weavings, and ceremonial cloth were now filthy and unkempt, smeared with the hearts of mosquitos and germs that spilled everywhere. Maggots, worms, and flies woke from their slumber at the foul odours, swarming around to partake in the spillage.

At the palace far away on Gunung Ledang, Dang Raya Rani was cajoling the Princess to drink milk, as always.

'Milk! Milk! Every night you give me this milk! Don't you know, old nanny, that I thirst for blood? Blood! Didn't you hear me? Blood!'

The Princess flew into a rage and stomped her feet so hard on the chamber floor that her glossy thick hair, which cascaded around her body, surged like the waves of the sea.

'Uh . . . uh . . . uh . . . magic stone, sweet flower stalk, umbrella of the diamond mountain . . . have patience. Tomorrow, surely, the emissaries from Malacca will arrive bearing the royal dowry . . . surely, they will bring two bowls of blood, no?'

The Princess smiled, seeing Dang Raya Rani's face so tender with love. And the Princess fantasized about drinking two bowls filled with the blood of Sultan Mahmud and his prince—sweet, salty, and hot! And how mouth-watering!

Watching the Full Moon

Last night was the fourteenth night of the moon. Tonight is the fifteenth, the night of the full moon. It's been a long time since we watched the full moon. And so, as twilight approached, when the sky was turning indigo in the west, we prepared to go to Teluk Bayan to watch the rising moon. We brought along a tikar mat and a torch. We packed light snacks like biscuits, ground nuts, and popcorn, as well as a few bottles of mineral water.

We walked down the Bayan Lepas highway that was built on reclaimed land along Teluk Bayan. To our left, the bay was calm, shimmering in the sunset. The last rays of the sun cast a golden-yellow palette over the leaves and trees of Jerejak Island. To our right, the sun was sinking behind the Bukit Relau hills. After a while, the warm golden glow grew murky and dim.

As we arrived at the edge of Teluk Bayan, the horizon in the east was glistening pale yellow and blue. A soft beam of light falling on the sea created a radiance that stretched from the source of light in the distance to the shore of the bay.

We spread out our tikar mat and sat facing the horizon that merged with the sea. The vivid sunset grew more and more resplendent. Then, slowly, the curved edge of the moon appeared, shining bright over the surface of the sea. The visible part of the moon gradually became larger and brighter. In a few brief moments, the moon rose to its full splendour—round and enormous, adorning the sky with its pure light, so brilliant that one could see the contours of a map within it.

The surrounding sea sparkled in yellow, white, and silver. The entire sky was lit in topaz yellow and sapphire blue. Before we knew it, the moon had risen a few feet above the surface of the water. We were overjoyed.

We looked around us, to the left, to the right, and behind. Suddenly, we saw that the entire beach was teeming with thousands of people, sitting in pairs on the rocks, on the sand, on motorbikes by the roadside, and by the seaside. They were all embracing while watching the moon.

'All those people . . .' observed my son. 'They are like sea lions on the coast of Siberia on National Geographic . . .'

'Yes, like sea lions, seals, and the elephant-headed-fish, Gajah Mina,' I replied.

What my son said was true. Couples were swarming for miles and miles to the north and south. Who knows where they had all come from?

As the moon rose higher, our vision was flooded with a soft whitish-mint glow. The sky was incandescent. We could not see a single star, only a faint flickering here and

Watching the Full Moon 87

there in the moonlight. But we clearly saw all the people around us, entranced, dressed in all styles and colours of clothing. We were absorbed in watching them.

When we looked back at the moon, we noticed a cluster of pitch black clouds emerging from the horizon, about a metre below the moon. The jagged peak of the clouds rose higher and higher. It morphed into the head of a giant dragon, complete with a pair of antennas protruding from its brow and a cockscomb along the spiky base of its neck. Soon, we saw the dragon's mouth open wide, baring its fangs as it moved towards the moon. Little by little, the moon entered the dragon's mouth, starting from below—a quarter, then half, then three quarters, until, at last, the moon was swallowed whole. The sky above was suddenly empty, yet bright and crisp. In an instant, the entire eastern shore was plunged into darkness. We were anxious and frightened.

'Let's go now,' I said.

We quickly packed our things and turned around to walk to the pavement. We switched on our torch. Oh, God! Our torch illuminated couples copulating, right there in the open.

'Ma!' my son cried.

'Come here!' I told him.

We couldn't find any room to make our way to the pavement. We shone our torch around us, but only saw people—thousands and thousands of them—having sex. Some of them had sprouted horns like bulls and buffaloes, some had grown tails like monkeys, some had fangs like

88 An Ordinary Tale About Women and Other Stories

lions and tigers, and some had become vipers, slithering and twisting. Snorts, howls, and groans pierced the air, mixing with the fishy odour of the sea.

We dragged ourselves along. We felt as if we were walking on smooth stones covered with moss, as if mushy and warm snakes were coiling around our calves. When we flashed our torch below us, we realized that we were stepping on the tummies and placentas of babies, covered in fluid and blood. And coiling around our legs were umbilical cords, still hot and dripping with mucus.

We shone our torch around us.

Oh, God!

Thousands of babies were simultaneously being born and dying.

The rocks were moving and shifting, and black gravestones were springing up everywhere. Then, the sand, earth, and stones started to crack—thousands of devils and demons crawled out of the open graves. They surged upward and forward, wearing tattered white robes, their faces smeared with blood, the flesh on their faces decomposing, their eyeballs bulging out of the sockets, their mouths only jawbones and teeth.

The devils and demons were coming towards us. We ran and ran. Who knows how many baby corpses and placentas we crushed underfoot. We just ran in the direction of the pavement.

'Ma!'

My son fell, stumbling on a copulating couple whose legs had turned into huge serpents.

Watching the Full Moon 89

'Get up!' I yelled.

I dragged my son up and ran. We sensed that we had reached the Bayan Lepas highway. But we felt hands pulling at our clothes from the back. Turning around, we saw that the devils and demons were right behind us and were springing up all around us. We kept running, but the Bayan Lepas highway had become strange and unfamiliar. There were no signboards. We had no idea where we were going.

'Just run!' I said.

The darkness grew darker. We couldn't see anything, and even less if we didn't shine our torch. Suddenly, we found ourselves in a small residential area.

'Papa . . . how could you do this to us . . .' We heard the moans and cries of a few young girls.

'What's wrong if I do this to you . . . you are my daughters. Rather than other men, it's better if I do it!' We heard the gruff and hoarse voice of an adult man.

'Papa can marry any woman, you don't need to do this to *kakak*, to me, to little Minah, to little Limah. Papa is tainting all of us . . . what will become of us?'

We heard the young girls sobbing.

'Where am I supposed to get the money to marry again? Your mother died without leaving a cent to look after all of you. I work hard to support all of you . . . what's wrong with taking some repayment? It doesn't even hurt . . . it's nothing . . . what's the matter then?'

'Papa is supposed to protect us. What will happen if we get pregnant?'

90   An Ordinary Tale About Women and Other Stories

'Your elder sister got pregnant once . . . nothing happened. If I could strangle her baby, I can strangle yours too. Just bury it below the house or throw it in the garbage can. Stray dogs will devour it clean in no time.'

'Come . . .' I said. 'I think there's a mosque over there.'

I dragged my son. We ran aimlessly, falling and stumbling many times. We got up again and kept running in the deep dark—the sky and earth and everything in it had become the blackest black.

We trampled babies who had been dumped, scattered all over the place. When we flashed our torch, we saw— some had no arms, some had guts spilling out of torn bellies, some were headless, some were nothing but a stub of flesh. Many times, we tripped over people who were copulating. And, in the torchlight, we saw that some of them had grown hairy like bears and some of their faces had morphed into monkeys and pigs. We even stumbled over a giant man, thoroughly engrossed in raping babies.

All of a sudden, we saw a small glowing light ahead of us. We headed in its direction. It turned out to be the light of a projector, emanating through a hole below the window of a concrete house. The projector was screening a series of pornographic clips for spectators of all backgrounds—old, young, men, women, some still in uniform. They filled a large hall to the brim. At the end of each series, they all revelled in a wild orgy in the open hall.

Peering through the same hole, I saw a room in the house brightly lit with cameras at every angle, filming naked people having sex in all positions. In another room,

Watching the Full Moon

we saw people producing pornographic movies, stacked in reels all the way to the ceiling. In the front yard of the house, we felt the rumble of a vehicle approaching in the dark. A door opened, casting a spiral beam of sinister light. We saw people loading thousands of film reels into the vehicle. When it was full, the vehicle sped off, and another one took its place.

'Come here!' I cried, yanking my son away.

We ran aimlessly until we reached a wall. When we shone our torchlight on it, a signboard appeared with the words: Religious Department. It was a tall eight-storeyed building, completely dark and silent. To the right, there loomed a magnificent structure—the grand gateway displayed the name: Jamek Mosque. We looked around the mosque, but everything was dark, silent, and stiff. Its doors and windows were latched and bolted.

By the walls of the mosque, we stumbled upon people with faces morphed into dogs, bears, and pigs, copulating like beasts.

'O God. . .' I muttered. 'How long this night is.'

'There's no place left for us to go. Let us just keep going. Perhaps the night will soon break into day.'

Then, we stopped running and started walking.

Watching the Rain

I once felt a sudden desire to watch the rain. I stepped onto the veranda and stood there facing the wide-open sky, grand in its expanse. To the east, the sky was veiled by dark grey clouds, nearly black, their billows gathering in layers. Each layer of cloud unfolded in countless monstrous shapes with jagged edges and rugged terrain—contoured, fragmented, swiftly transforming.

My son came to stand beside me, clad in a red round-necked sweater and matching floppy hat. The cool wind began to blow fiercely. Yellowish *angsana* leaves tossed about in disarray on the roadside as the wind swept them to the west. The crests of casuarina trees rose up, obstructing the darkening sky as their lithe bodies swayed to and fro. In horizontal flight, a flock of doves flapped against the wind, passing in front of the brooding clouds.

The charcoal-coloured clouds moved briskly westward. There, we could see the Relau mountain range shrouded in mist, as if held captive by the solemn sky. The mountains held their breath, silent, yet hopeful and poised, anticipating the arrival of rain in restless pleasure. Far below, in the

94   An Ordinary Tale About Women and Other Stories

front yards of houses across the street from ours, lush casuarina and mango trees also awaited the rain, brimming with tranquil excitement. As the wind surged wildly, leaves of ochre, pale yellow, and deep green swirled and scattered in all directions.

Rain began to fall in a trickle. We were overjoyed. The trickle grew heavier and heavier. Gusts of wind whipped the rain into the verandah where we stood, splashing our faces till we were soaked. We both laughed, my son jumping up and down in delight.

As the rain poured down in torrents, the tops of the casuarina trees became murkier and almost disappeared. The Relau mountain range, too, was hardly visible now. The storm raged so violently that we soon had to retreat inside, closing the door to the verandah.

'We can't watch the rain anymore from the verandah,' said my son. 'What shall we do now, Ma?'

'Let's go to the clouds, how about that?' I replied.

'Yay . . . we are going to the clouds!'

My son leapt with joy.

'Come, help me make our wings,' I told him.

'Wings?'

'Yes, wings.'

We went to the storeroom and gathered the feathers of the *jentayu* bird that we had collected from the seashore some time ago. We carefully went to work sewing and glueing, until we had crafted two pairs of sturdy wings. Small wings for my son and larger wings for myself. We fastened the wings to our bodies.

Watching the Rain 95

'Remember, Idat,' I said, 'don't fly too far from me, always stay by my side, don't fly behind me.'

'I'll remember, Ma,' he replied.

We soared through the rain, ascending towards the clouds. At last, we alighted on them, seated giants heaving in their vastness that stretched into the indigo horizon. In the west, the sun cast its evening glow, lining the clouds' silhouette with a dazzling yellow-white shimmer.

We were filled with joy. Leaping from cloud to cloud, we played hide-and-seek, my son crouching behind a mound of grey clouds while I searched for him. Once I found him, it was my turn to hide. Laughter filled the air as we chased each other through the billows. We tossed ourselves high into the air and let ourselves tumble through the thick, fluffy clouds. Then, we rolled around until we reached the end of the expanse.

Standing at the tip of the colossal clouds, we saw the red-gold sun slowly sinking, gilding the sky in a thousand shades of splendour. As the sun disappeared from view, we turned around to find ourselves cradled by millions of sparkling stars strewn across the sky.

We ran back again. We soared upwards to touch the stars hovering around us. My son plucked a few small stars within his reach and stuffed them into his sleeve. Some stars fell into the clouds, swirling and glittering like diamonds on dark blue and deep red velvet lit by neon lights.

As we bent down to pick up the fallen stars, my son let out a cry of astonishment.

96   An Ordinary Tale About Women and Other Stories

'Ma! Look down there, people are playing with fireworks everywhere. Is tonight the celebration of Hari Raya, Ma?'

'No, my love . . . no, they aren't playing with fireworks . . . those are bombs going off in Sarajevo. If we were there, we would be witnessing the massacre of Bosnians by Serbian soldiers.'

'And over there?'

'Those are gunshots among warring groups in Somalia, Rwanda, South Africa, and several areas of the African continent.'

'And what about over there?'

'Those are Israeli snipers aimed at the Palestinian people in the West Bank.'

'And down here?'

'That's crossfire from the conflict in Cambodia. And over there is the war in Afghanistan.'

'It looks like people are fighting in every corner of the earth, Ma . . .'

'Yes. Every day we hear and watch another war unfolding . . . The world is critically ill, human beings no longer want to look after the world.'

'How do we stop these wars, Ma?'

'We don't have the power to do that, my dear. War, killing each other, the lust for power, greed—these are human pastimes in our age.'

'Ma, what if we set traps and catch the leaders who make war and put them all into an iron sack, then we throw them into the Qulzum Sea near the middle of the Lake of Pauh Janggi, and we let the Garuda bird eat them all . . .'

'We could, but we don't have traps or iron. Anyway, even if we catch one of those leaders, ten more will emerge.'

'Like aliens, Ma? Like *critters* . . .'

'Yes . . . something like that . . . as I said, war is their pastime. It's not enough to make war on others, they even make war with those of their own religion, with their own siblings, there are even children who make war on their parents. When something is a pastime, that's how it is.'

'If there's war everywhere in the world, the air will become so dirty, right Ma? We don't have to return to our home then, right Ma?'

'Yes, we'll just stay here.'

'Ma, you don't need to return to the university?'

'No.'

'Why not?'

'There's war there too.'

'War?'

'Yes, a cold war between justice and discrimination, between brown-nosers and little napoleons, it's a place where the promotion of employees is a scarcity.'

'Don't you want to work somewhere else, Ma?'

'It's the same in other places. Human beings have become sheep who only follow a shepherd . . . they are envious, treacherous, mocking . . . money hungry, power hungry, position hungry.'

'Will we live here forever then?'

98   An Ordinary Tale About Women and Other Stories

'Yes, forever.'

'Yay!'

My son bounded in delight. Together, we ran and gathered stars until our sarong sacks overflowed with their wondrous radiance. Lost in our star gathering, we barely noticed dawn breaking overhead. With our sacks full, we continued walking westward, carrying our precious stars with us.

When we looked back, we saw the sun scaling the sky. And unfolding before us—vast deserts, undulating and exposed. We marvelled at how swiftly time had brought us there. Suddenly, we found ourselves in front of an Arab woman, clad in a black niqab, gathering pebbles and dry leaves. Nearby, a chubby baby boy slept soundly in the shade of a large rock. Just a few yards from the baby's feet, a clear, tranquil pond shimmered.

'Good day,' I said.

'Good day to you,' she replied.

'I am al-Zuhra,' I said. 'And this is my son, Adil Hidayat. We just happened to pass this way. What is your name, madam? Why do you choose to live here?'

'Al-Zuhra?'

'Yes, al-Zuhra.'

'I am Hajar, the wife of Ibrahim. That's my son, Ismail. I am forced to live here.'

'Subhanallah, come with us to a better place.'

'No, thank you. This is our home. We are happy . . . we are content despite this suffering and misery. One day, this place will become a magnificent city. People

Watching the Rain

from all corners of the world will come to drink from this small pond, mark my words. We single mothers are destined to endure great and bitter trials in this life. Yet, we gather and multiply our strength from the resilience of others.'

'It is true, since your era until today, the world is still disrupted by the presence of single mothers.'

Hajar served us Zamzam water in a bowl-shaped stone.

'Thank you, madam,' I said. 'I wish you a pleasant day.'

'I wish you the same.'

We pressed on, journeying further and further away from Hajar and her son Ismail.

After several sunrises and sunsets in the desert, we arrived at the outskirts of an oasis, in a distinctly different landscape. Here, tall date palm trees stood, their green leaves trembling and laden with fruit. We saw groves of olive trees, and pomegranate trees with fruits ripening to a rich crimson. We came upon a pond surrounded by bushes bearing small yellow flowers. Nearby, among rows of date palms, we saw a humble stable made from palm bark and leaves. Inside, a beautiful young woman wearing a veil was nursing a baby boy. We approached her.

'Good day,' I said.

'Good day to you too,' she replied.

The woman lifted her head from her baby to look at us.

'I am al-Zuhra,' I told her. 'And this is my son, Adil Hidayat.'

She stretched out her hand and we exchanged greetings.

'Al-Zuhra?'

100   An Ordinary Tale About Women and Other Stories

'Yes, al-Zuhra. Your son is beautiful.'

'Yes, but so is yours.'

'Indeed. Why do you choose to live alone here? I mean, alone with your son?'

'My name is Mariam bint Imran. This is my son, Isa. I gave birth to him without a father. My people cursed me, so my family hid me away here.'

'Subhanallah, come with me to our place. We can live there together.'

'No, thank you. This is our home. We are happy in this suffering. One day, my son will become a Prophet of God. He will spread the word of the true religion. Remember, we were born to be single mothers; suffering is our fate. This fate is cheerfulness and joy for a single mother.'

'How true, Mariam bint Imran.'

We drank the water and ate the dates that Mariam served us. Then, I took my son's hand, and we continued our journey.

'Are we going to watch the rain again, Ma?' my son asked.

'Yes, we will watch the rain again.'

'Where?'

'In a place that's peaceful and calm.'

'Where?'

'Here, among the clouds.'

Narration of the Ninth Tale

After performing Asr salutations, reciting dhikr, and offering prayers, Raja Malik ul-Mansur stepped out on the terrace. He sat on the balustrade, leaned against the engraved wooden fence, and gazed out at the Manjung river. The water appeared clear and calm, its ripples sparkling in the evening sunlight. Across the river, white sand stretched along the banks all the way to the estuary. In the distance, one could see the attap roofs of houses nestled among coconut palms and fruit trees. The evening breeze caressed Raja Malik ul-Mansur's face—mild, cool, melancholic.

Three years had passed since it all happened. It was around that time when the people of Manjung gathered at the wharf of the Manjung river to welcome Raja Malik ul-Mansur as he arrived by boat from Pasai. The Chief of Manjung invited Raja Malik to his home, where he could serve his sentence of exile or live out the rest of his days. Memories of Samudera, of Sidi Ali Hisyamuddin, and every aspect of his former life were still a source of bitterness and pain for him.

Tears of regret streamed down Raja Malik ul-Mansur's cheeks, soaking his lap before falling to the ground, watering the grass and weeds. The earth and grass were submerged by the salty fluid, which flowed into the Manjung river, causing it to swell. The sparkle of light on the water's surface disappeared, giving way to an untold sorrow—gloomy and profane. Fish, frogs, and prawns floated to the surface of the water, shedding their own tears of sadness, while the overgrown sedges and knot grass along the riverbank momentarily lost their vibrant green. Leaves and twigs across the Manjung river grew pallid, drained of their golden-yellow glow.

In the front yard of the Chief of Manjung's house, a tangle of worms squirmed their way out of the soil, flushed by the hot tears that had started to trickle into the earth's crevices. A large and long eelworm surfaced in front of the stairs and peered over the puddle of tears. The first thing the worm saw was a pair of eyes—the wellspring from which tears now surged.

'Baaaaah,' cried the worm. 'Such a deluge of tears, pouring non-stop. If this continues, where will our children and grandchildren go? Why won't this man go and weep his eyes out in the jungle, somewhere uninhabited by delicate animals and insects; why here of all places . . .'

Raja Malik ul-Mansur heard the words of the eelworm and felt utterly wretched and despicable.

'Worm,' said Raja Malik ul-Mansur, 'have you ever been a ruler, a conqueror in your world?'

Narration of the Ninth Tale   103

'No, I have not. However, I am the prophet of all worms. I have come to see with my own eyes the catastrophe that has befallen my kind. They just sent an emissary to seek my help. This hot flood will surely wipe us out, we shall be scalded by your tears. What is it that so pains you, Raja Malik ul-Mansur?'

'I have committed evil, I did not heed the advice of my old servant...'

'Evil... evil... a weary dilemma that has never been resolved by humankind who has been tempted by Satan ever since God created Adam and Eve from a clump of earth. Love and affection, embodiments of desire and lust, often lead to evil, the loss of humanity, hatred, and vengeance. O Raja Malik ul-Mansur, such temptation led to Adam's expulsion from heaven, his separation from Eve, crossing seas and deserts. Agamemnon left his troops stranded at Aulis for ten years and sacrificed his own daughter to rescue Helen from the Trojans. Menelaus' extreme love for his wife Helen of Argos led to countless deaths and the sacrifice of the great warrior Achilles. Ah, just as Adam committed evil, defying God's command out of love for Eve, you too have erred by your human nature. Stop your tears now, or my kind will perish in this simmering flood.'

Raja Malik ul-Mansur wiped his eyes with the seamed dyed cloth draped over his shoulder. Yet his tears still flowed incessantly.

'Truly, I am full of remorse, o prophet of the worms,' Raja Malik ul-Mansur murmured as he gazed out ahead.

104 An Ordinary Tale About Women and Other Stories

'I am a human being, supposedly a higher creature than your kind. Yet I am more wretched, for I have forsaken faith and honesty. How difficult it is to uphold that faith . . .'

Just then, Raja Malik ul-Mansur saw a cloud of immaculate white mist drifting above the trees across the Manjung river. The clump of mist floated closer and closer to where he was sitting on the terrace by the wooden fence. As it approached, Raja Malik ul-Mansur was startled and delighted to see the face of Sidi Ali Hisyamuddin, looking at him with sad and limpid eyes from the nebulous cloud suspended in the sky.

'My loyal steward, we must go to Pasai . . . we must survey the state of our brother's kingdom. Who knows in what state it lies since he was captured by Raja Syahrunawi.'

'My lord, do not go there, if you do, slander will befall you . . .'

'Ah, how could that be . . . why would slander arise simply by going to survey a kingdom?'

'Slander lurks in every place and time, seizing even the faintest opportunity. Like a spider in its web, it lies in wait, ready to ensnare. Just as flies, mosquitoes, and gnats are trapped in the web's silken threads, unable to break free, so too do the powerless fall prey to slander's grip. If only they could grow stronger and shatter the web with a single stroke. But alas, they remain fragile insects, doomed to be devoured by the sly spider.'

Raja Malik ul-Mansur sighed as he listened to the prophet of worms. Then he looked at the face of Sidi Ali

Narration of the Ninth Tale 105

Hisyamuddin, still shrouded in mist, his sad eyes a mirror of his eternal purity and unconditional loyalty.

'I am full of remorse, old steward,' said Raja Malik ul-Mansur. 'If only I had foreseen the terrible consequences. But then, my mind was shrouded in layers of impenetrable walls. I persuaded the young maiden to return with me to Samudera. How enchanting she was, like a fairy offering her soft white arms. Her smile was like a split pomegranate dripping sweet nectar, veiled by the undulating waves of her thick black tresses cascading in curls down to her hips. Ah, she was a sparkling gem of desire!'

'For three years you have been dragged by your age and experience, o Raja Malik ul-Mansur. Three years is not a short period of time. Yet, you are still haunted by your wrongdoing. Don't you remember Menelaus, who fought so valiantly to rescue the abducted Helen—ten years later when he finally won the war and brought Helen home, he noticed that Helen's hair had turned white and that her face was no longer as pristine as marble. Where did her beauty go, o Raja ul-Mansur?'

Raja Malik ul-Mansur looked into the shining eyes of the prophet of worms, who cast a pitiful gaze at him. He bowed his head and saw that the palms of his hands were wet with tears.

'It is all over,' muttered Raja Malik ul-Mansur, who was between listening and not listening. 'Everything has happened by the will of fate. Now I am the prisoner of my brother, Raja Malik ul-Tahir. It is he who holds power over

106   An Ordinary Tale About Women and Other Stories

my life now. Why won't he just kill me and release me from the regret and disgrace of this illusory world?'

Then the prophet of worms lifted a veil of the sky to reveal a vision.

'Look,' urged the prophet of worms. 'Behold, Raja Malik ul-Mansur.'

Raja Malik ul-Mansur saw himself on the palace grounds of his brother, Raja Malik ul-Tahir. As a criminal condemned to severe punishment, he stood with his head bowed, eyes fixed on the ground trodden by countless feet. His shame felt as vast as the universe. Even the cackling of toads from a pile of old logs in the corner of the palace garden seemed to mock him. How difficult it is for a man awaiting a death sentence to muster the will to live. Beside him stood Sidi Ali Hisyamuddin, his head also lowered. This elderly man had vowed to the late Sultan Malik ul-Salih to remain loyal and protect him. Now, he suffered for another's crime. Why had fate subjected such a noble man to such a humiliating end?

At this moment, the Grand Vizier Tun Perpatih Tulus Tukang Segara flashed a sinister smile, eyeing the captive men like Maalik Zabaniah, the archangel at the doors of Hell.

'Because of your vile character, I dethrone you. You are now my prisoner,' declared Raja Malik ul-Tahir. 'Not a single one of your warriors knows that you and your servant have been captured. You are forbidden to return to your kingdom or to remain here in my kingdom. I shall exile you to Manjung.'

Raja Malik ul-Mansur could no longer defend himself or Sidi Ali Hisyamuddin. Everything had happened so quickly. That morning, he had been invited to Pasai to attend the royal circumcision ceremony of Raja Ahmad, the prince of Raja Malik ul-Tahir. He had accepted the invitation out of respect for his elder brother. But only Raja Malik ul-Mansur and Sidi Ali Hisyamuddin were allowed into the palace; his warriors were prohibited from participating in the ceremony.

Now, his warriors all waited outside the palace, with no idea of what was taking place inside. What a wretched turn of fate. Perhaps even more wretched than the fate of Raja Malik ul-Tahir himself, who had once been captured by Raja Syahrunawi and forced to work as a poultry farmer.

'Take him to Manjung immediately!' Raja Malik ul-Tahir commanded.

Raja Malik ul-Mansur breathed a sigh of relief that he was not to be immediately executed. Yet what difference would it make, in the end?

'And you,' Raja Malik al-Tahir now addressed Sidi Ali Hisyamuddin. 'You remain here. You are not to follow Raja Malik ul-Mansur. If you follow him, I shall order your execution now!'

His hands tied behind his back, Sidi Ali Hisyamuddin did not offer salutation but nodded his head at Raja Malik ul-Tahir.

'I would sooner my head be severed from my body than be separated from my master.'

108   An Ordinary Tale About Women and Other Stories

With a single stroke, Sidi Ali Hisyamuddin was beheaded. His head fell and rolled onto the grass, thick red blood spurting from his neck and severed head. His blood flowed between the tufts of grass and seeped into the earth of the Pasai kingdom—it mingled with the dust and splashed onto the vines adorning the palace fence, and it dripped from the end of the sword of Raja ul-Tahir's general, staining the shiny blade a murky dark red.

Raja Malik ul-Mansur saw all of it. He watched the headless body collapse to the ground, landing with a thud on the grass and dirt with hands still tied behind its back. He saw Sidi Ali Hisyamuddin's head roll towards his feet, facing the sky with eyes closed tight. Amid the stream of blood still gushing, soaking the hair now splayed out on the grass and dust, he could almost discern a faint smile on the severed head's mouth.

Even now, his wrongdoing had not yet been atoned for. His penance was not over, even though his tears deluged the coast of Manjung.

'My generals! My warriors!' Raja Malik ul-Mansur exclaimed while shaking his head. 'They did not know that their king was captured. Why did they let it all happen . . . they should have ambushed the soldiers of Raja Malik ul-Tahir, they should have sacrificed themselves to defend the dignity of their king. They should have lined up their bodies to make a bridge for their king to cross the river! Ah, my dishonourable warriors! They were silent, utterly powerless to protect their own king!'

Narration of the Ninth Tale

The prophet of worms then drew down the veil of the sky that had revealed the vision of all that had happened. And the veil descended all the way down to the earth and dissolved into the flood of Raja Malik ul-Mansur's tears.

'Your own dignity . . . haha . . . why should anyone else defend your dignity, o Raja Malik ul-Mansur? Until when do you wish to use others as a tool to defend your dignity? Aren't you a king? Shouldn't a king be a king in all aspects? A true leader? If you are no more than a baby freshly out from your mother's womb, it would be better for you to offer your kingship to someone else or stretch out your neck to be beheaded by your enemies if your kingdom comes under siege!'

'O worm! Have you never experienced the carnal desire that was planted by God in humankind?'

'Why not? If there was no carnal desire, how would we breed and beget our descendants?'

'But your stature and condition is so different from us human beings! We have so much blood to be spilled, flesh to be torn to pieces, bones to be scattered.'

'And so you make this earth a site to erect your memorial stones? Do you want to stain the earth's surface with your blood, your bones, your flesh? Uh! Humankind has gone mad, completely mad . . . drinking their own blood and tears, licking the pus from their wounds, eating their own shit, devouring their own bones and flesh! Even the cursed devil does not eat its own flesh and blood! Uh!'

At that very moment, a dirt path overgrown with bramble suddenly started moving and rumbling. The prophet of worms craned his neck as high as he could to take a good look at the moving dirt path. Raja Malik ul-Mansur turned to look in the same direction.

'They are coming!'

The prophet of worms cried, startling Raja Malik ul-Mansur.

'They . . . who?'

'Your path to freedom!'

And the prophet of worms slinked into a hole in the earth, disappearing beneath the pool of tears.

'Who is that?' asked Raja Malik ul-Mansur. 'Who are they?'

The prophet of worms popped his head out again, just enough to peer over the flood of tears.

'Don't you know, o Raja Malik ul-Mansur, that fate came calling to Icarus who stubbornly defied the orders of his father Daedalus? Don't you know that the glue that binds your wings has melted in the scorching rays of the sun and your wings are now falling, feather by feather, into the sea beneath you? O, you will never reach the island with your father; soon you will fall deep into the black sea, you will sink in your obstinacy! Farewell, Raja Malik ul-Mansur!'

'You have determined that the hour has arrived for me, what strength do I have to elude the power of fate?'

Then several men came into sight, wearing the uniforms of Raja Malik ul-Tahir's court, well-known to Raja Malik ul-Mansur.

Narration of the Ninth Tale

'The hour has come . . .'

Raja Malik ul-Mansur dabbed his tears and looked in the direction of the approaching soldiers, the blades of their upturned spears glistening in the evening sun.

Now, they stood before the steps where Raja Malik ul-Mansur was seated. He addressed them: 'Has an order arrived from my brother, o subjects of Pasai?'

'Yes, my lord,' replied one of the soldiers. 'We have been ordered by His Majesty to invite you to return to Pasai . . .'

'Can't you just carry out my punishment here in Manjung? Or does my brother's thirst for vengeance remain unquenched?'

'No, my lord, we are not here to carry out punishment. We have been ordered to invite you to return to your kingdom . . .'

'What has caused my brother's change of heart?'

'Realization, my lord. . .'

'Realization?'

'Yes . . . His Majesty realized that his attitude was foolish—because of your minor wrongdoing, you have been exiled from your kingdom and your kingdom has been captured, just because of a maiden . . .'

'Is that true?'

'It is true, my lord.'

'I do not wish to set out today. Dusk is almost upon us. Let us begin our journey at dawn tomorrow, so that we may arrive at Samudera before midday. Come up and spend the night here, we will rise while the morning is still dark.'

112   An Ordinary Tale About Women and Other Stories

As a single streak of dawn appeared above the orchard in the eastern sky of Manjung, Raja Malik ul-Mansur prepared himself for the Fajr prayer. Raja Malik ul-Tahir's men were already stirring from sleep and arranging the belongings of Raja Malik ul-Mansur to be carried to the boat at the Manjung wharf.

Once all the preparations were complete, the Chief of Manjung and a few dignitaries accompanied Raja Malik ul-Mansur to the wharf. Raja Malik ul-Tahir's men were already waiting in the boat.

'Thank you for your kindness towards me during my time here. May the Almighty repay your good deeds.'

The Chief of Manjung and his dignitaries offered a royal salute to Raja Malik ul-Mansur, their hearts aching with pity for the exiled king. Only now, after three years in exile, Raja Malik ul-Mansur felt like a king again, who may live beside a blade of grass that sprouted overnight in silence.

The oarsmen thrust the vessel out to the middle of the Manjung river. It slowly steadied itself along the spine of the water and began its journey upstream to Samudera. The wind blew from behind, propelling the boat forward as it veered left and right, navigating the currents at the surface of the Manjung river.

'I want to stop for a while at Padang Maya,' Raja Malik ul-Mansur told the soldiers, who understood his intention.

'We will arrive at Padang Maya soon, Your Majesty,' replied one of the men. There's just one more bay to pass before we reach it . . .'

Narration of the Ninth Tale 113

Raja Malik ul-Mansur remembered how he leaned over, watching the drops of water softly shatter against the hull of the boat. A few drops landed on his lap and left wet stains on the samping cloth wrapped at his waist. Indeed, the water's character had not changed since he had arrived three years ago. In the splash and spray of the water's shining white froth, one of the boatmen suddenly cried out. A human head was bobbing in the water, fast approaching the hull of their boat now heading to Manjung.

'There's a head drifting in the water!' exclaimed the boatman.

Then, Raja Malik ul-Mansur saw the boatman plunging his own hands into the water to fish out the human head.

'O, God! My loyal steward, Sidi Ali Hisyamuddin, has followed us all the way here!'

Raja Malik ul-Mansur's tears flowed freely into the river, merging with the current that wound its way around Padang Maya. He remembered everything—how he, a king blinded by lust, had caused the beheading of one of his most loyal and honourable stewards. And that head, severed from its body, now followed the king's boat by the power of the Almighty, unnoticed until it emerged floating next to the boat as they approached Padang Maya.

'Padang Maya! Let us stop here for a while,' said Raja Malik ul-Mansur, once he had ascertained that the human head upon his lap was that of Sidi Ali Hisyamuddin. 'I want to give the corpse of my loyal steward a proper burial here. Are any among you willing to help me to request from my brother, Raja Malik ul-Tahir, the body of Sidi Ali Hisyamuddin that lies in Pasai?'

The men, awestruck at the power of the Almighty, stirred out of their stupor.

'I am willing to make that request, my lord . . .'

114   An Ordinary Tale About Women and Other Stories

'Very well, go quickly. Leave me here with some of your men.'

As the sun was disappearing behind the mountains in the west, Raja Malik ul-Mansur completed the burial of Sidi Ali Hisyamuddin's corpse—its head now reunited with its body. The body that had willingly offered itself to death now rested peacefully in the eternal land, the final destination that awaited him.

Kruuuukkk, kruuukkk, kruuuuuuukkk—the oarsmen rowed. *Celuummm, celaammm*—the long oars plunging into the water. Raja Malik ul-Mansur slowly slipped out of his own body, transforming into an invisible bird, soaring to survey the universe that now felt estranged to him.

Samudera, yes, Samudera. The worldly riches that had been passed down as inheritance by his late father— in the name of love, as an entrustment, a pledge, and an obligation to be guarded with his body and soul and bones and blood—who knew what condition it was in. All had been lost; everything had grown distant. The people of Samudera had been ruled by a king for so many years only to suddenly see their king utterly humiliated. What strength remained in each drop of blood, each cut of flesh, each bone of the people of Samudera, to help their former king ascend the throne? Certainly, they had forgotten the king they had once so revered. How would they accept his return? How? A good king is a king adored; a bad king is a king deposed. Now that he had been deposed, would they revere him once more?

'Dark and empty . . .'

The oarsmen paused upon hearing incomprehensible muttering and listless sighs from Raja Malik ul-Mansur.

Narration of the Ninth Tale 115

A few moments later, they resumed rowing, shaking their heads.

'Of what worth is a king if he has no subjects?' The oarsmen laughed in their hearts, and thought: 'A king is worth as many pairs of hands are raised to foreheads in royal salutation of Daulat Tuanku . . . if not a single pair of hands is raised, he is no better than a dead wooden stump . . . a bramble, just a nuisance . . .'

The oarsmen glanced at Raja Malik ul-Mansur and found him gloomy and mournful. A black-grey cloud was passing before his eyes.

'Ah, we have arrived at Padang Maya, my lord,' announced the helmsman. Raja Malik ul-Mansur lifted his head and looked towards the shore. He saw the green plains that stretched from the shore all the way to the edge of the jungle. And he saw the grave of Sidi Ali Hisyamuddin, embraced by a wooden tombstone that still looked solid although it had been exposed to heat, dew, and rain since it was laid there three years ago. No shrubs or weeds had sprouted on the grassy patch around it, the only grave in the field. It was as if the burial of Sidi Ali Hisyamuddin had happened just this morning.

Raja Malik ul-Mansur knelt before the grave of Sidi Ali Hisyamuddin, both his hands upturned as he offered prayers for the soul of his departed loyal steward. Then he wiped his face with both hands, bowed his head and contemplated the grave, overcome with sorrow and guilt.

'I shall take leave now, *bapak*. Stay here in peace . . . I have been invited to return by my brother . . .'

116   An Ordinary Tale About Women and Other Stories

'Where else do you wish to go, Your Majesty . . . this is the finest place for you . . .'

Raja Malik ul-Mansur was momentarily stunned by the voice that spoke to him from the grave of Sidi Ali Hisyamuddin. Then he stood up and walked to the edge of the river. The boatmen were already holding the ends of the log bridge for Raja Malik ul-Mansur to cross. But instead, Raja Malik al-Mansur bent down to perform *wuduk* ablution. He then walked back to the grave of Sidi Ali Hisyamuddin, unfurled the head cloth that was draped across his shoulder, and spread it out on the grass next to the grave of Sidi Ali Hisyamuddin. Then, Raja Malik ul-Mansur performed two *rakat* of prayers.

'Assalamu'alaikum warahmatullah . . .'

After the final salam, Raja Malik ul-Mansur lay down on his cloth at the side of the grave of Sidi Ali Hisyamuddin.

'What is the matter with the king?' asked one of the boatmen holding up the log bridge.

'He wishes to rest a while,' replied the helmsman.

'Can't he rest here? It's not as if he does any work on this boat . . . The faster we climb aboard, the faster we will arrive! This king is nothing but a nuisance!' grumbled another.

'Perhaps he expects us to escort him to the boat, like an official royal ceremony! Hahaha!'

'Let me go and have a look,' said the helmsman, getting up. 'It seems as if he has fallen asleep there, what a rascal this king is!'

The helmsman was rather surprised to see how soundly Raja Malik ul-Mansur slept, his body completely

Narration of the Ninth Tale   117

unmoving. The helmsman crouched beside Raja Malik ul-Mansur and gently patted him on the shoulder a few times.

'My lord, it is time for us to leave.'

Raja ul-Mansur's body felt rather weak and limp to the touch of the helmsman.

'My lord! My lord!'

The helmsman shook the king's body more firmly this time, but Raja Malik ul-Mansur remained limp and lifeless. He then felt Raja Malik ul-Mansur's wrist—there was no pulse. He placed his palm over Raja Malik ul-Mansur's heart—there was no heartbeat. He placed his forefinger under Raja Malik ul-Mansur's nostrils which were almost still like a person deep in slumber—there was no warmth of inhaled or exhaled breath.

'Hey, come here quick, all of you!'

All the boatmen hurried to the shore and came to the spot where the helmsman was crouching before the body of the king.

'Raja Malik ul-Mansur has departed,' declared the helmsman.

'Departed?'

'Wasn't he fresh and well just moments ago?'

'We thought he was sleeping . . .'

'Ah, how easy is his death! We all thought he was just resting after prayers!'

'Some of you, go and deliver the news to His Majesty Raja Malik ul-Tahir. Some of you stay here and guard the corpse of Raja Malik ul-Mansur.'

As dusk fell, the grass and weeds of Padang Maya were trodden on by countless slaves, elephants, and horses that arrived as part of Raja Malik ul-Tahir's ceremonial procession to the funeral rites for his deceased brother, Raja Malik ul-Mansur, beside the grave of Sidi Ali Hisyamuddin. During the nights that followed, heavy dew fell to revive the wilted field.

The Lovers of Muharram

The Angel of Paradise stands at the crest of Mount Sinai. The Angel of Paradise wears a robe of satin, shimmering dove grey. The Angel of Paradise holds a shiny black staff, hewn from a branch of the tree of heaven.

And the sun of the last dusk of the month of Zulhijjah casts its yellow-red-gold rays over the green grass and the large rocks and the small white, pale blue and pink daisy flowers and over the leaves of the tree of heaven, finally falling on the robe of the Angel of Paradise and on his hair that cascades in brown curls to graze his shoulders.

Now, a gentle cool breeze is blowing. And the leaves of the tree of heaven quiver and surge with life as they rustle, sighing to each other, and some sway and turn upside down. A lustrous glow emanates, reflecting the sunlight that scatters on the leaves of the tree of heaven, pale green and velvety.

Only now appear two leaves of the tree of heaven that are still pristine, unmarked by any inscription.

The Angel of Paradise is surprised. The Angel of Paradise takes his staff and walks towards the leaves of

120   An Ordinary Tale About Women and Other Stories

the tree of heaven. Tok-tok, tok-tok, the sound of the tip of his staff striking against the rocks that cradle the crest of Mount Sinai.

It seems as if these two leaves of the tree of heaven have germinated and sprouted only a few moments ago. Or could it have been an unintentional oversight, since these two leaves are concealed by dense foliage? Should these two leaves be left as they are until dawn arrives on the first morning of the month of Muharram?

The Angel of Paradise turns around and faces the west. The flaming red-gold rays of the evening sun saturate the sky above the desert, unfurled in its ochre vastness. He sees the panorama of the sprawling city all the way to the grey-blue sea. And the walls of the city have turned parchment-yellow in the dusk. Ships glide, their funnels releasing black smoke into the evening air. He sees the pinnacles of skyscrapers strewn against the boundlessness of the galaxy. He sees the interconnected network of telegraph wires. He sees the labyrinth of bridges and roads. He sees countless vehicles criss-crossing in all directions. He sees people moving like swarms of ants. He sees everything. He sees all.

Along a road somewhere outside a city in the west, there is a wanderer. His stride is vigorous and he looks straight ahead. And along a road somewhere outside a city in the east, there is a wanderer. Her steps are steady, her gaze fixed firmly before her.

Does each wanderer sense the existence of the other? Where is the end of each of their journeys? Do they intend

The Lovers of Muharram 121

to keep wandering until the end of the last night of the month of Zulhijjah?

Through his senses, the Angel of Paradise approaches the wanderer outside the walls of the city in the west.

'Where are you going, Sir?'

'I'm searching for something.'

'What are you in search of?'

'A companion.'

'A companion for what?'

'For life in this world and the next.'

Then the Angel of Paradise leaves the wanderer outside the city in the west and approaches, through his senses, the wanderer outside the city in the east.

'Where are you going, Miss?'

'I myself do not know.'

'How long will you wander?'

'I myself do not know.'

'Don't you want to stop somewhere to rest?'

'I myself do not know.'

'Doesn't this kind of wandering only bring disquiet?'

'I myself do not know.'

The Angel of Paradise breaks a twig of the tree of heaven that dangles close to his brow. Milky white sap oozes from the twig's stump, dripping onto the green grass and the large rocks scattered below the tree of heaven.

The Angel of Paradise dips the snapped-off end of the twig into the beads of sap on the stone. The Angel inscribes the first Arab letter *sin*, followed by the letter *ya*, then the letters *dal* and *nun*, and then *zal*, until the letters

122   An Ordinary Tale About Women and Other Stories

form the complete name of the wanderer outside the city in the west.

Again the Angel of Paradise dips the twig of the tree of heaven into the beads of sap and inscribes another letter below the name of the wanderer outside the city in the west, starting with the letter *pa*, then the letter *alif*, then the letter *ta*, until the letters form the complete name of the wanderer outside the city in the east.

The Angel of Paradise carefully regards the letters inscribed on the leaves of the tree of heaven. These two leaves are now engraved with the names of the two wanderers he had encountered through his senses.

The Angel of Paradise smiles. He is pleased with the result of his work. The other leaves of the tree of heaven rustle gently in the twilight breeze. And the sun of the last dusk of the month of Zulhijjah sinks away into the desert horizon in the west and the western sky billows into wondrous variegated clouds.

Now I am on my way to the small town of Sindalaya, southwest of the city. And I hope I can return before nightfall.

As I pass through the small town of Langsala, I remember that there are no cigarettes left in my tobacco case. On a lone journey like this, one of course needs something that can help the senses focus on the road and the meandering vehicles all around.

I stop my car at the roadside, right in front of a row of shops in the town of Langsala. And now I am about to cross the street to one of the shops.

The Lovers of Muharram

I see her standing by a pushcart vendor selling peeled fruits. Her blouse is black. Her sand-coloured sarong is patterned with a pair of brown eagle wings. A black belt, two inches wide. A pair of black sandals, partially concealed by the hem of her sarong. She wears a plastic ivory-coloured pearl on a red plastic arm-cuff. And a red bag with long straps hangs from her shoulder.

From a distance, I caress her arms and shoulders with my gaze. How smooth and bare in the overcast late afternoon. And I stroke her hair. Thick black hair, ending in curls, cascading to the left and right of her chest and flowing down her back.

She's tall and a little plump, her body looks as if it has been formed by the dexterous hands of a classical sculptor.

As she moves on to another fruit vendor, I want to grasp her arm. I go into a shop and buy cigarettes, then I smoke a stick and continue watching her.

Now she is buying a papaya and talking to the fruit seller. I approach her from behind.

'May I ask you something?'

'Yes? Oh, what?'

'What a large papaya you are buying . . .'

'Ah, ya . . .'

She takes the papaya, which she has placed in a plastic bag, holding it with both arms together with a tin of powdered milk.

'Your husband didn't come with you?'

'Husband? Me? Oh . . . ha . . . ha ...'

'Do you have a husband?'

'Who needs a husband when one can live alone?'

'Is that so? May I ask . . .'

'Yes?'

'Ah, can we go over there to my car across the street?'

'Let me put these things down in my car first. Are you a student? Do you want to ask me about an essay?'

'No . . . where's your car? The blue one?'

'No. The green one there.'

'This one?'

'Yes.'

'Then let me talk to you here for a while. Ah, now it's drizzling . . . may I come into the car?'

'You may. Nah, come in.'

'Where are you going after this?'

'To buy something for dinner.'

'Where?'

'Over there, at that little restaurant.'

'Why don't you eat with me at that restaurant?'

'Thanks, but I'm afraid I won't make it back before Maghrib prayers are over.'

'Are you so pious?'

'No. Just fulfilling my obligations to God.'

'Where do you live?'

'12 Minden Heights . . .'

'Job?'

'That's the place and address of where I work, in front of you. Read it.'

'Oh! Is that the full name?'

'Yes.'

The Lovers of Muharram

'I'm Syed Nazri . . . just call me N if you like.'

'Nice to meet you . . .'

'Such soft hands . . . what lotion do you use?'

'Formed by nature.'

'Oh! This car isn't good for you. It's steering is rigid. Your hands will become callused. Also, there's no air-conditioning. Your body will constantly sweat and become hot and sticky . . .'

'This is my first and last choice. It's not my problem if others like it or not.'

'There's a car that wants to overtake. You better move your car out of the way.'

'I don't have a right to do that. Those who come first, go first. Those who come later, go later. Why should someone else always give way?'

'Ah . . . you defeat me. Oh, is this your photo?'

'Yes.'

'What landscape is that in the photo?'

'On the island of Langkawi.'

'Ah, this sentence . . . *In a crowded world, I only have myself.* What does it mean?'

'You don't understand it?'

'Is it true that you are all alone in this world? Father, mother, siblings?'

'My father is deceased. My mother lives alone in the village. I have three older sisters in the village too.'

'You are the youngest?'

'Yes.'

'Would you allow me to accompany you in this world?'

126   An Ordinary Tale About Women and Other Stories

'I would, thank you.'

'Will you go out with me tomorrow?'

'Where do you want to take me?'

'For a meal, for a walk, to look at the sea . . .'

'Where should I wait?'

'Here. I'll come at half-past seven in the evening. Surely you would have done your Maghrib prayers by then.'

'All right. I want to go home now . . .'

'Okay. Ah, your face is opening sweetly . . . just now I could only give marks to your ass . . . to your waist . . . to your breasts . . . to your arms . . . to your hair . . . now I can give marks to your face too . . . ha ha ha!'

'How many marks would you give to all those spots you mentioned?'

'Your ass: eighty five . . . waist: eighty five . . . breasts: eighty . . .'

'Enough. Is this the worth of a woman in the eyes of a man?'

'I'm trying to be honest. That's truly what my heart felt when I approached you . . .'

'All right. Let me go home now.'

'See you again. Ah, the palm of your hand is hot . . . good night. Tomorrow, ya?'

'Hmm hmmm.'

Shall I describe the loneliness of being deserted by a lover like the loneliness of a shore suddenly deserted by the waves? Or the desolation of a mountain suddenly stripped

The Lovers of Muharram

of all its vegetation, until not a single green leaf or blade of grass remains?

Until now, I do not know where Abdullah is. Abdullah has really disappeared. Abdullah no longer calls to ask me out for lunch. Abdullah no longer takes me out every Saturday night. Abdullah no longer brings me to the beach every Sunday to watch the waves.

And Abdullah no longer cares how I feel. Abdullah is dead. How tormenting it is, Abdullah's sudden absence. I'm bewildered. Unhinged. I hardly know what to do anymore.

God, how grateful I would be if You could let me encounter Abdullah again at a five-foot way, or a crossroad, or at the edge of any public space!

Now I have come to the small town of Langsala, without any specific intention of buying anything. I want Abdullah to catch sight of me in a public space.

Only now I remember that there's no milk powder left at home. And there are no fruits left in the fridge since this morning. So I might as well buy some fruits, now that I've strayed into Langsala.

As I bargain over a papaya, the sky grows overcast. The evening sun has vanished behind the peaks of the Bukit Bendera range. And I still harbour a hope that Abdullah will suddenly appear before the rain.

He comes. Not Abdullah. A sturdy man. Honey-dark skin. Fine curly hair. A thick moustache. He has a slight belly and stands a few inches taller than me. He wears a long-sleeved shirt with narrow stripes—yellow, light

128   An Ordinary Tale About Women and Other Stories

green, pale red—in the style of *Come September*. And dark grey trousers.

Who is he? I feel that I have seen him somewhere. Have I met him before? When? Where? An off-campus student? A police officer? Who is he?

Now, he is asking me some trivial questions. And now, he is walking on my right, accompanying me to my car. A whiff of fragrance drifts over from his body now and then, carried by the dusk breeze. I can hear the click-clacking of his shoes, his steady footfall against the gravelly street in the town of Langsala.

And now, he enters the car to sit beside me. I hear him chuckle three times. And I see him grin a few times. His voice is somewhat rough, hoarse, its tone full of teasing.

He says my car isn't quite right here and there. He says my car is inappropriate. It will need to be replaced after two–three years of use. Its metal rusts easily. Its engine has been assembled locally. They put in a compact engine that's difficult to repair if any of its parts malfunction.

'I'm thrilled by your ass,' he says, 'I want to tell you how many marks I give for your ass . . . your breasts . . . your waist . . . I'm captivated!'

'You're crazy!'

'Yes, that's right! If I had looked at your face first, I surely wouldn't have been this crazy. Perhaps I wouldn't even have come to talk to you . . .'

I ask God whether this man is a devil or an ordinary, cruel human being. I'm shocked that he behaves so strangely. I'm appalled that I met him.

The Lovers of Muharram 129

I'm hurt by how he humiliates my being. Deeply offended. Silently, I bury my rage to take revenge on him tomorrow night. In God's name, I will strike back at him with all my resentment for every word he uttered. What a pig he is! What an ape!

I did not come to Langsala to meet him. I came to look for Abdullah. Or I came in search of a little calm and a little preoccupation to fill my vacant heart.

'Tomorrow night, I want you to wear something sexier than what you are wearing tonight . . .' he says.

'Why can't you just accept me as I am? Why should I do what you want?'

'So that you'll look sexier . . . more seductive!'

'It's night already. I want to go home.'

'Tomorrow night, then?'

He takes my right hand and kisses it for a few moments. In his eyes I see a glint of lust, caught in the light from the restaurant across the street. I feel a soft heat on the back of my right hand.

Night arrives with a lingering drizzle. And I feel uneasy and disgraced and guilty for having met him.

Who is he? An off-campus student? A police officer? A devil? A djinn? Why did God make me meet such a cruel person?

Did he send his spirit two days ago, in the shape of a yellow butterfly with white and blue-grey dots, to perch on my shoulder?

We are the sky-thrusting trees in this botanical garden. We are the ones who watch the sun return every evening to its sanctuary beyond the

130   An Ordinary Tale About Women and Other Stories

crest of the mountains. We are the ones who see the sun at daybreak rising above the face of the eastern sea.

And we are the ones who witness the vows of lovers. And we are the ones who hear the promises of love. And we are the ones who taste the scent of love's flesh in the flowers that scatter from us.

Now, we watch the last sun of the month of Zulhijjah disappear behind the mountains. As the moist night wind rustles our leaves and branches and tendrils, we move and rub against each other in the secret solitude of the hushed night. And darkness enshrouds our existence in the colour of night.

Among the cars resting in our shade along the roadside, something is new tonight. Perhaps it is a newness that will arrive with the month of Muharram?

Two people are walking. Holding hands. There are whispered words, indistinct. There are words of seduction, flirtatious and playful. They stop under our branches.

'I'm so glad I met you. I've always admired women with beautiful bodies, but I never imagined I would be with one of them.'

'The other day you said my face wouldn't earn a score. How can I walk beside you without showing my face?'

'There's nothing in you that is lacking . . . everything is more than enough.'

'You know how to seduce women . . .'

'I'm just being straightforward . . .'

'Why did you bring me here?'

'You've never been here before?'

'I have. But never on night like this.'

'I want to tell you a secret.'

The Lovers of Muharram

'What?'

'That evening, I did not observe you from head to toe.'

'Then?'

'I looked at you from the tip of your toes to the ends of your hair.'

'I did not see shadows. I looked straight into you.'

'And what happened then?'

'I immediately loved what I saw . . . I felt I had found what I was looking for. When I look back on my past, I feel regret. I have never received love or affection from anyone. Once, when I lay in hospital for a week, not a single woman came to visit and bring me flowers . . . if I fell ill again, would you come to visit me?'

'Of course I would. As long as you die when you see my face.'

'Ah, don't strike me again. Tell me you love me.'

'So fast? We just met a few nights ago . . . love and affection must be cultivated; it can't just explode like a balloon.'

'It can. Love can explode in our hearts like a balloon.'

'That's just fantasy.'

'No. My love for you has exploded like a balloon . . . I want to make you my wife . . . are you willing?'

'Ah, wait. Don't rush like that. I don't even know you . . . maybe you're a drug dealer . . . maybe a robber . . . who knows. I don't want to marry someone I don't know. Furthermore, I don't like anything about you yet.'

'You don't even like one thing about me?'

'Only your shirt. I like your shirt.'

'Thanks . . . you seem to be having your revenge . . . you want to take me down the way Muhammad Ali takes down his rivals.'

'Good if you feel that way. Who are you really?'

'Oh, God . . . this is my deepest secret . . .'

'So, you really are a drug dealer . . .'

'For God's sake, don't accuse me with such contempt. Nah, here's my identity card . . .'

'It's dark, how can I even see it?'

'Wait, I'll light a match . . . there, look . . . you see?'

'Oh, so you are?'

'Yes. Please keep my secret.'

'In that case, I feel safe with you . . .'

'Do you love me?'

'I love you . . .'

'Do you want me?'

'I want you . . .'

And we witness the two bodies slowly sway and fall to the earth among our roots and to eternity. And we hear the dry fallen leaves that cover the earth crackling at the touch of hair and fingers. And our roots recoil momentarily from the heat of a woman's breath. And we scatter small flowers to cover her bare breasts.

As the last night of Zulhijjah reaches its end, they rise as a pair of lovers who have just scaled the crest of the mountain range in the west.

And we know the secret mischief of the Angel of Paradise. He is surely sound asleep now upon his heavenly divan.

The Lovers of Muharram 133

I am standing on my balcony looking at the mountain range in the west. There is no sun. But I can see its rays casting beams of light from the mountain into the evening sky, and the clouds forming resplendent, breathtaking colours.

That's when I see her coming, walking into the compound of our house from the main street. She's wearing a dark grey sarong and a sleeveless black halter neck blouse, and she's carrying a deep blue umbrella. Her arms are bare in the evening light.

'Hi! Pat . . . it's been ages since you visited . . . is it a dream? Come up, come up . . .'

I run down from the balcony and stand before her. And I see her eyes are bloodshot and glistening, and her face is sullen.

'How are you?'

'Just as you see me, of course. I'm well . . . fine . . . and you? Are you ill? Come upstairs first . . .'

Pat sits with her legs dangling from a yellow plastic chair on the balcony facing the mountains. She looks as if she is dreaming of a past happiness.

'Is your family not at home?'

'Abah is in the back room, resting. Mak is out with my younger siblings . . . My brother is playing badminton at the club. Why, Pat?'

Pat is still gazing at something in the distance, towards the crest of the mountain. I do not know what she is looking at because I don't see anything at the top of the mountain, except a formless greyish blue.

134 An Ordinary Tale About Women and Other Stories

A few months ago, Pat came to this balcony wearing a red sleeveless blouse, a white sarong skirt and a white scarf fluttering from her neck.

I still remember Pat running like a young *kijang* deer, to hug me on the porch. And I remember Pat's cheeks were flushed with a joy that she could not conceal, brimming from her heart.

'Ti,' Pat said, 'I'm happy. I'm overjoyed. He truly loves me.'

'Ah, congratulations, Pat . . . finally you've met someone who you love, and who loves you . . . congratulations. How do you know he truly loves you?'

'We've already discussed our wedding. We've discussed how many children we want.'

'Ho ho! How many did you say you want?'

'I want them all, girls, boys, half a dozen, a dozen, it doesn't matter . . . but he only wants two sons. He says if we have two children and they are both girls, he won't want me to give birth again. He would rather adopt—'

'Ah, I'm getting scared listening to you, Pat!'

'Ah, you don't known . . . it gets even scarier . . .'

'Tell me!'

'He always holds and kisses me in front of his friends . . . he doesn't care anymore if he wants to kiss . . . he keeps telling his friends to ask me if I love him . . .'

'Eiii, the hair on my neck is standing . . .'

'You know what he did last night?'

'Hah, what?'

'There were four of his friends sitting with us at the park facing the sea. He took off my shoes and put my feet

The Lovers of Muharram   135

on his lap. I was so embarrassed. People passing by looked at us and laughed. I left him and walked barefoot towards the sea. Do you know what he did? He followed me and carried my shoes all the way . . . ah, he's really crazy . . . like a monkey with an egg, not knowing what to do with it . . .'

'I am happy for you . . . look after his heart. This time, I hope it lasts till the end of time!'

'I hope so too. He always says he won't forget me till doomsday. He always asks me to tell him I love him . . . asks me to think of him . . . ah, I feel so glorious now . . . I feel that God has given him to me as a new year gift . . .'

Now Pat's cheeks are no longer flushed. Her lips are shut tight, quivering as if they are hiding a terrible secret. I hear Pat sigh three or four times, still gazing at the mountains in the west that are fading fast in the evening light.

'Pat . . . why?'

'You want to be burdened with this secret?'

'In the name of Allah . . . I will keep it to myself alone. What is it?'

'Look at my belly . . .'

'Hmm, why?'

'Do you see anything?'

'No, it looks normal . . . just a little fuller . . .'

'I am carrying his child . . . almost five months now . . .'

'Subhanallah! *Astaghfirullah!* When will you marry?'

'What point is there to marry . . . it's not as if you don't know, I've been living in his house . . . he says a marriage certificate is nothing but theory . . . a receipt to buy a woman . . .'

136   An Ordinary Tale About Women and Other Stories

'But what about his child, then? Don't you know that such a sin will be borne by the child down to seven generations? What if your child is a girl . . . when she's old enough to marry, what will others say when she takes a *wali raja* because she has no male guardian related by blood?'

'I'll try harder . . . has your mother ever mentioned anything about a concoction to abort a pregnancy? Or have you heard of anything?'

'No. They don't discuss that openly . . . you yourself know that they treat me like a child because I'm not yet married . . .'

'I don't know . . . I'll keep trying . . .'

'I once read . . . some people eat unripe pineapple . . . some drink the water of the *celaka* root . . . visit a traditional midwife. . .'

'I've tried everything . . .'

'Isn't he helping you?'

'He wants the child to live . . .'

'Then quickly get married!?'

'How can we? I'm not a Syarifah, not a descendant of Syeds. He is a descendant of Syeds. His parents have already said they don't like me. He certainly won't throw away his parents because of me.'

'Oh, God . . . Can I go see him now or tomorrow, before your pregnancy advances?'

'See him?'

'Yes . . .'

'You . . . you know where he is now?'

The Lovers of Muharram 137

'Where?'

'I don't know . . . he hasn't been home for a month . . . he said he has some things to settle in KL . . . not even a letter . . . no news . . . I asked his friends, none of them know anything . . .'

'*Ya Rabbi* . . . Do you think he has left you?'

'I think so . . . the only clothes he left are the ones he doesn't wear . . .'

'How are you going to hide your belly at work later?'

'I have already given notice of resignation at the end of this month . . .'

'*Ya Rabbilalamin* . . . how are you going to live?'

'I am applying for a job at a firm . . . maybe I'll get it . . .'

'What if you don't?'

'I'll become a first- or second-class whore . . .'

'No, Pat. Don't . . . if you don't want to be ashamed of yourself, think of your mother, or your family, at least think of me . . . don't, Pat!'

'Hahahaha . . . I'm just joking. I'm sorry, Ti. I still think of God . . . I still pray . . .'

'Now?'

'No . . . I stopped praying since I moved in with him . . . no fasting either . . . just this Friday I started praying again . . . I was so awkward . . . I feel ashamed before God . . .'

'Why?'

'What's the point of praying? If the fridge is full of whisky, brandy, beer, baby champ, pink lady . . . and whatever else . . . night clubs every week . . . wallowing in

138   An Ordinary Tale About Women and Other Stories

zina . . . what's the point of praying, of fasting . . . I don't want to be a hypocrite . . .'

'What about your house rent?'

'He paid this month's rent already . . . next month I will leave.'

'Where will you stay?'

'I don't know . . .'

'I'm afraid to live, Pat . . . I'm afraid to listen to your story.'

'It's good if you are afraid. I am far too bold. Till I see lions as meek goats . . . let me go now . . . don't worry about me . . . I feel lighter now after talking to you. Tomorrow or the day after, I'll come again, if you aren't ashamed to see me . . .'

'Come, Pat. Come. I feel sorry for your misfortune . . .'

Pat leaves. Her silhouette disappears around the street's curve into the twilight. I see the crest of the mountains in the west looming in the darkness like a sleeping demon.

On this terrible morning, everything is relentless—a downpour from a sky heavy with grey clouds, soaked leaves and water dripping everywhere, branches and twigs now refreshed with rain.

Almost all the young ones of the troop are nowhere to be seen. Who knows where the infants are taking shelter: under which branch, at the base of which trunk. Who knows at which root the offspring are now cradled, in which hollow. The lingering quiet is broken by a long screech, kreeeeeiiiiiiih, in the middle of the jungle towards the top of the hill.

The Lovers of Muharram

Eeeeeeeeiiiiikkkk . . . Again, the long-drawn-out screeching. Once. Twice. Three times . . . and all the young ones emerge and jump in the direction of the sound. From all corners the infants tumble out, chattering boisterously. The branches are shaking in commotion, sending rain drops scattering onto the leaves.

'Who is causing such unrest? Kreeiihhh . . . kreeiiihhhh . . .' 'Is it the troop from the other side coming to attack us again? Kreeeiiihhh kreeiihhh . . .'

Now, all the young ones have gathered, paying no attention to the rain and the drops of water on their backs. The offspring do not care that their fur is soaked. Kreeiihhh! Their black tails dangle close below their abdomen.

Eeeeeeeeeeeeeiiiiiiikkkkkkkk!

Uuuu . . . uuu . . . kreeiiiaaaaahhhh!

Uuuu . . . uuuuuu!

Now, everyone is jumping at the top of the hill, towards a grove of large trees.

'Uuuuuu! Uuu!'

Now, the male chief reaches the branch of a seraya *tree and tells us all to stop. We all stop. The young ones are all drenched.*

'Uu! Uu! Uuuuuu!' The male chief cries out, his muzzle pointing ahead. And he shakes the tree with both hands a few times, furrowing his brow and widening his eyes, 'Uuuuu! Uuuuu!'

And we see it. All the infants come close to gather on the rain-wet branches.

A young woman is tossing on the earth by the gnarled roots of a meranti *tree. Her arms are flailing, her legs twitching. Her clothes are soaked through. The dry leaves beneath her are smeared*

140 An Ordinary Tale About Women and Other Stories

with red fluid. Between her thighs, a little creature is moving and shrieking.

'Eeeeeiiiiikkkkk! Eeeeeiiiiikkkkk!'

'Uuuuuu! Uuuuuu!' It cries out again.

Now the woman slowly gets up. She wipes herself with a cloth stained with red patches. Then she wraps the little restless creature in the cloth. She stands up and tries to walk, staggering while clutching the giant roots. She doesn't look at us. Her face is almost covered by her thick black dripping-wet hair.

'Eeeeeeeiiiiiiikkkkkk! Eeeeeeeeiiiiikkkkkk! Eeeeeeeiiiiiii kkkkk!'

She doesn't turn around. Slowly, she clambers down the rocky chasm, grasping at twigs and roots. Then, she vanishes.

We start leaping. The branches shudder and rain drops scatter onto the leaves.

'Uuuu! Uuuuuu! Uuuuuu! Kreeeeiiiiikkkkkk.'

'Uuuuuuuuuuu!'

'Kreiiiiiiaaaaaahhhhh!'

'Uuuuuuuuu!'

The male chief climbs down to the soil by the roots of the meranti tree, where the little creature lies. The male chief tears open the swaddling cloth, rummaging with both his hands. The female chief runs over and snatches the cloth, ripping it to pieces. Shreds of cloth are now strewn over the leaves here and there.

'Eeeeeeeeiiiiiiikkkkkkkk! Eeeeeeeeiiiiiiikkkkkkkk! Eee eeeeeiiiiiiikkkkkkkkkk!'

The cry of the strange, restless creature is shrill. The female chief kisses the face of the little creature. The male chief pulls at one of its

The Lovers of Muharram 141

arms. Their offspring arrive. Each of them pointing with their muzzles, dangling from the branches, and crunching dry leaves underfoot.

Now, all of them reach out to touch the strange shrieking creature. More and more young ones gather around. Some pull at its eyelids. Some squeeze its nose, others pinch its ears. Some tug at its hair. Others pull at its fingers and toes. Some pull the cord that runs from its navel and is attached to a mushy object flung upon the dry leaves.

Suddenly, a young one bites the cord from its navel until it ruptures. The strange creature emits a long, deafening cry. Another young one bites its fingers and chews them off. Another bites its toes and chews them off too. More young ones come and sink their teeth in.

Now, the strange creature's screams are bloodcurdling as it flails the stumps of its hands and feet. Another young one digs at its eye and plucks it out. And the little creature stops shrieking and is silent. Another young one bites its ears and gnaws them both off. Another tugs at its arms and rips one off. Yet another imitates his friend in delight, it yanks at a leg and rips it off.

Soon, the strange creature is nothing more than some pieces of flesh strewn here and there over the dry leaves. Its stomach and liver and spleen are scattered here and there. And a sweet-sickly odour fills the air, mixed with rainwater and the scent of decaying leaves.

By evening, the rain has stopped. We carry the story of the strange creature everywhere. And all the trees, the stones, the streams, all the insects and worms cackle in laughter at our tale.

We heard the story from the monkeys in this botanical garden. The terrible fate of a human creature, set in motion by two lovers who rose from half-sleep among our roots on the last night of the month of Zulhijah.

142 An Ordinary Tale About Women and Other Stories

'Angel of Paradise, emerge from your divan of slumber. All the water that fell to earth this morning were nature's tears for a baby who was born beyond its will.'

'Trees . . . although I was the one who brought them together, you gave them shade to sleep among your roots. You serenaded them, lulling them to fornicate in the obscurity of your forest . . . I now proclaim that all your leaves shall no longer bear new shoots. And your leaves shall decay, and your green shall no longer renew itself. Wither away, until Hari Kiamat, the Day of Judgement. Wither away . . . Wither away . . . And your twigs shall no longer flow with sap or nectar . . . take heed, you shall soon become rotten tree stumps . . .'

'Angel of Paradise! We are not at fault! The children of Adam are at fault! We were not created for them . . . we are for the monkeys, the caterpillars, the birds! Not for the wretched children of Adam, do not curse us!'

'With your withered barrenness, may the children of Adam find no place for romantic encounters . . .'

We see the Angel of Paradise amble to the crest of Mount Sinai. He stands beneath the tree of heaven and tilts his head, observing all the leaves rustling in the wind of this overcast evening.

'Stay, all you leaves of the tree of heaven . . . stay pristine in your original state . . . I shall no longer inscribe the names of the children of Adam upon your skin.'

We see two teardrops fall from the eyelids of the Angel of Paradise, roll down his cheeks, then finally fall upon the large rocks scattered by his feet, and the rocks shatter into tiny stones.

The trees beside me now weep, lamenting their tragic fate, condemned by the Angel's curse to eternal decay.